The Boys of My Sun
The World Takes, ,D
Because, The Tr
LeeRoy Jordan, Jr.
p. cm.

ISBN 978-0-578-48225-5
Registration #: TXu 2-137-138

Effective Date of Registration:
February 21, 2019

Jacket design by Toussaint Jordan

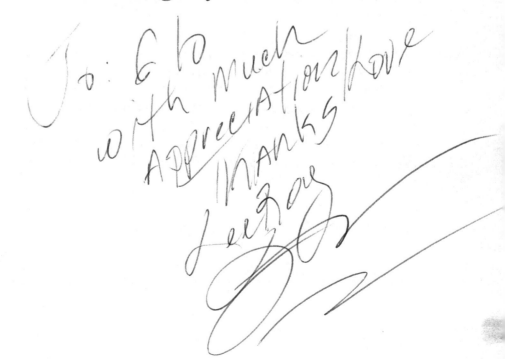

To: Elo
with much
appreciation/love
thanks
LeeRoy

"Trenton Makes The World Takes"

The Truth Is Spoken Here

By

LeeRoy Jordan, Jr.

Forward by

Once Upon A SummerTime I have a Dream
To Go Tell It On The Mountain, on a hot, quiet
Summer Nights, After The Rain, By The Fire Next Time,
with My Baby, My Girl, Sweet Sue
Around Midnight, with Nhima, In A Mellow Mood, with Monalisa, on
Cloud Nine, with Stella By Starlight
The Candy Man Can, yes, I Thought About You, The Way You Do
The Things You Do, Unforgettable and How Sweet It Is To Be Loved
By You
My Funny Valentine –You Send Me, Higher and Higher, By Any
Means Necessary, so I Just Wanted To Stop And Thank You Baby

Ain't No Mountain High Enough, Ain't No Valley Low Enough for A Native Son, call me by my Rightful name – MR. Bojangles
Watching from the Watchtower, Sitting On The Dock of The Bay
Accused of Whistling in Mississippi and maybe in Jasper Too
Old Man River, Why Should White Guys Have All The Fun
Oh How I long forty years for, Yesterday
When All My Troubles Seemed So Far Away
Ain't it Peculiar, Ennis, What Happens to A Dream Deferred?
After Donald Writes No More
In Soledad brothers were we but now we're blind and can't see
Tupacalypse Now
All Eyes On, Me, Against The World
Through Misty, Purple Hays
Notorious Big and Blood In My Eye

"Hey LeeRoy, Yo Mama, She Calling You Man"
By LeeRoy Jordan

Introduction

This book is written in dedication, it is written with inspiration, tribute, profound sadness and the virtue of hope. It is written for and about a city and the aftermath of what has become of too many of its sons. It is written about a city in America - and the abbreviated lives of more than two hundred of its sons - *"The Boys of My Summers."*

The following pages is a treatise born out of the writer's life and the lives of the "boys 2 men" who he grew up with - "boys 2 men" whose lives were all too brief. "Boys 2 Men," who died too early, too soon and too young.

These pages are written with a profound sense of longing, bewilderment, love and in loving memory of each of them and our childhoods and growing up in the capital city of New Jersey, where there is a bridge spanning the width of the Delaware River which exclaims in its illumination into the night skyline – it declares, that "Trenton Makes, The World Takes."

It is a book written as a labor of love. It is written for my children – those living (Le'Sean and Toussaint) and the spirit of two sons (Lamar and LeeRoy) who are deceased yet still alive in me.

Obviously there have been many texts written about the plight of African American boys and men, the social scientist have dissected our mental and physical being. We have been labeled an "endangered species."

We have been the subject of literally thousands of articles and studies that examine our condition as the male of the race to which we belong. The intentional interpersonal violence and the incarceration rates that incapacitate so many of us has been the subject of many books, articles and television documentaries. We have been the subject of movies like "Boyz N The Hood" a movie that received critical acclaim as they testify to the pathology of violence and murder that consumes our very existence and the aftermath of "continuing traumatic stress" it leaves on the families and communities that we leave behind. I have learned much from many of the books that have been written and I have inspired me by authors such as Alfred "Coach" Powell (MESSAGE NA BOTTLE and THE SCANDAL CONTINUES, Volume II), Nathan McCall ("Makes Me Want To Holler"), and one of my heroes, Dr. Geoffrey Canada ("Fist, Sticks, Knives and Guns," and Reaching Up For Manhood"). I am forever indebted to Dr. Jawanza Kunjufu for his stellar work and volumes of "Countering the Conspiracy to Destroy Black Boys" and to Walter Beach III, who allowed me to walk next to him and work for him and being allowed to gain a pebble of the knowledge in his stellar book, "Consider This;" and the Reverend Dr. Alfonso Wyatt and Shawn Dove both who I have worked and collaborated and sought their advice.

This is not a feel sorry for black men book. And while it, like many of the treatise that I have and will refer to herein it will speak to our collective plight, this book is a "Call To Arms," to all of us who are still able to speak. This is a book that speaks to the tutorial of my teachers such as Dr. Ron Karenga the architect of Kwanzaa, who encourages us "to bear witness to the truth, to place the scales of justice in their proper place, among those who have no voice."

Preface:

Black Boys and Men: Dying Not for A Cause But Because

There is a passage in the Holy Bible, which springs from Job, 14th Chapter, 1st Verse; "A man born from a woman is here but a few days and full of trouble," that speaks to the contemporary plight of "black males; boys and men, living and dying in America. As aforementioned, these pages are dedicated to the lives of more than two hundred boys who grew up with the writer in Trenton, New Jersey and who died prematurely. But moreover it is written to make a statement; to shine a light, and to do something about the chronic epidemic of excess and premature death experienced by African American boys and men, their families, cities and a nation to which they are born.

On the day that a black male child is born in the United States, he can be expected to lead the most abbreviated life comparable to that of any other child not of his race or gender, born on the same day.

Black males, of which I am one, lead the nation in the rate of death for nearly all leading causes of death for the group to which we belong (heart disease, cancer, stroke, HIV, influenza and pneumonia, lower respiratory disease, unintentional injuries and adverse effects, motor vehicle accidents, homicide and legal intervention, diabetes, chronic liver disease and cirrhosis and chronic obstructive pulmonary disease and suicide of those 15-24.

We lead the nation in the rate of "Years of Potential Life Lost" (YPLL) before age 65 and are more likely to be murdered than any other segment of our nation's population and have the highest cancer incidence, the highest cancer mortality rate for all Americans and the highest prostate cancer incidence and mortality rate in the world. In recent years our suicide rates, especially among young black males, 15-19, have increased dramatically, to numbers that are unprecedented.

In another place, in the Bible, Psalms, 90th Chapter, 10th Verse, it says that "The days of our years are threescore years and ten……," The latter translates into 70 years, an age that as a group, black male infants; based on the most recent statistics on black male life expectancy (71.9), have only just begun to be experienced by us as a group and that based on our YPLL, most of us will never see. Psalm 90 goes on to read; "and if they be fourscore years, yet their strength labour and sorrow; for it is soon cut off, and we fly away."
There is no clearer description that I could have come up with that articulates the plight of African American boys and men than is found in these two pieces of scripture.

And if another truth be allowed to be told, in the United States of America Black Women; as a group, die before all other groups of women in this country. And when they have not died physically, parts and pieces of them die when their fathers, sons, brothers, uncles, nephews, husbands, cousins, fiances, and boyfriends die and thus they die with us.

The women of Trenton who have been in our lives were eyewitnesses, they were our siblings, they were our girlfriends, our childhood sweethearts, the mothers of our children, our wives, lovers, some of them our crime partners and best of all they were and still are our friends. They've been on the ride, the journey, with us nearly every step of the way and they still are. We loved and lived together, partied together, we went to the V Bar, the Fantasy Lounge, Paulie's Corner, the Babbling Brook, Scottie's, the Candlelight Lounge, the Crossing Inn, Charlie Harper's, the Turf Club, BT's Lounge, Black Jack's, Ray's Lounge and other places of dance and romance, drinking and other "thangs," including some of the best Cabarets on the planet!

Pam, Fox, Gwen and Motoe

Thus in memoriam I want to "call out their names;" the names of women who were here with us and whose lives ended too soon and sudden like the "Boys": Marcia aka "Marsha" Travers, Althea George, Alberta Garvin, Gwen Williams, Louise Berry, Priscilla Cummings, Linda Housley, Rita Washington and Sheila Washington and "Zetty."

Linda Housley (right)

GEORGE, ALTHEA
422 Walnut Ave.
Clerical
Voc: Business Ed. Teacher

Sissy, Pam, Delores Ann, Pearl, Sheila, Tanya

MY JUICY,
I MISSED YOU SUNDAY NIGHT and I'LL MISS YOU FROM NOW ON. RIP TYRONE GEORGE Rest In Peace

And thousands on top of thousands of us will pay into a system called Social Security, investing tens of millions of our dollars, which most of us, based on our rate of death and the ages at which we die, at best we may collect four years in checks. And based on the historical fact that we die younger than men in a third world country like Bangladesh; prior to our forty fifth birthday, most of us are paying into a system of which we will never receive anything. As compared to all other Americans, black males;

considering life expectancy, die almost ten years earlier than Americans as a whole. White women, the safest, healthiest gender/race group in America; as a group, live to be 80 years of age, outlive black males by nearly ten plus years. Black women and white men respectively live to be over 75 years of age and the nation as a whole lives to be nearly 79 years of age.

Our collective lives are cut short, in large measure, by causes of death that are preventable. We lose more than 100, 000 lives each year, of which nearly forty thousand is due to heart disease, and more than 30, 000 due to cancers. In the categories of cancer we lead the nation in the rate of death due to lung cancer caused by cigarette smoking, colon/rectal cancer, prostate and esophageal cancer.

In the case of prostate cancer, we die because we fail to get yearly prostate examinations and many of us fail to get examinations because we suffer from another disorder called "homophobia." We consider any rectal intrusion as an affront to our manhood and consider it a violation of such, to the degree that an examination or rectal intrusion, particularly by another man (i.e., a male doctor) is equated with and is considered, by many of us, an act of homosexuality.

Our death rate due to prostate cancer is also due to the misinformation we have received from the medical community over the years. Historically men have been advised to get their first prostate examination beginning at age 50, an age that is too late for black men. Only recently have the medical profession recognized that black men need to get a prostate examination at least 10 years earlier than their white male counterparts. In fact it is the writer's belief that we should be requesting such exams as early as age 30 and should be talking about it to young black men as early as age 15. And more often than not we die because we fail to be informed about preventive measures that could prolong our lives.

And as it relates to our sexual functioning we put a life threatening value on that of an erect penis. Thus those of us; and there are many, who suffer from hypertension, diabetes, and bad/high cholesterol, experience erectile dysfunction or "ED." Because of the value put on our being able to get and maintain an erect penis during sexual intercourse, when oftentimes we cannot, we opt to stop taking our medications; high blood pressure meds, resulting in stroke, a leading cause of death for African American men.

We die because of what we eat; processed foods, simple carbohydrates, high fructose and corn syrup, deep fried meats, and with whom and where we sleep. We die due to neglect, stress, internalized oppression and chronic self-induced-self destructive living and what we have failed and continue to fail to do to save our own lives. We die; as Joe Marshall – in his book "Street Soldiers" – of the Omega Boys Club puts it, of "Hood Disease-AIDS" ('Addicted to Death and Incarceration Syndrome'). We die because we don't love ourselves and we continue to die because we have become our own and our worst enemy. We have become all too willing to kill ourselves through homicide or suicide. We die living on islands of food desserts, genocidal-suicidal-homicidal-fratricidal-gendercide pathology and third world health care within a continent of first world affluence, spending shared time standing on a foundation of glass. Glass that is smooth and hard but when hit by a rock it shatters sending us down through the almost razor like shards soaking the fabric of our lives with our blood.

We die because we are spectators in our own war. To continue to be spectators is to be collaborators and conspirators in our collective demise. "Our people die for the lack of knowledge."

Chapter One

Setting the Context: The Life Expectancy of African American Males in the United States

Although excerpts of this book including its title have been contemplated, written and rewritten over more than a decade, its serious pinning began in true earnest shortly after the deaths of "Bernie Mac," at age 50 and Isaac Hayes at age 65. At the time of their deaths these two men represented more than just entertainment. Their lives embodied the relevant culture of America, hard work, persistence, perseverance, resilience, the belief in possibility, the willingness to pursue a dream and hard earned, hard won and honed talent.

Within a time period residing inside of two centuries; the 20th and the 21st, both Isaac Hayes and Bernie Mac reached tens of millions of us through their genius. They made us smile, dance, love, laugh, cry, made our hearts sigh. They made us feel warm and loving and proud of them and of ourselves. They exemplified the best in us – a credit to our race, community, our nation and their families.

While I, like a lot of us, I did not know either of them personally although it feels like I did. I mourned their loss like the rest of us – with a degree of sorrow and condolences to their families and their friends as did we all. But having done so and with all due respect to their lives these two kings, one of comedy and the other the rhythm of "sweet soul" and blues, were, at the time of their respective deaths, the last two people in the death line of African American males in the United States. Their deaths represent the all too common pathological occurrences of "excess and premature" death and the greatest number of YPLL compared to any other ethnic, race or sex group in our nation.

In fact, on the day that we are born in America, we can be expected to lead the most abbreviated lives of any ethno-cultural, racial or gender group in the nation. At the time of their deaths, Bernie Mac and Isaac Hayes had lived an average age of fifty-seven years of life. Among those African American men who reach the public's eye as they had, the story of their deaths are not atypical but rather typical of the brevity of life experienced by the group to which they were members.

Temptations:

Take into consideration the lives and deaths of one of the most dynamic and enduring groups of our times – "The Temptations" (Paul, Eddie, David, Melvin and Otis) who sang to us through the sixties, seventies, eighties, nineties and into the 21st Century. However, of the original five it was only Otis that crossed over into the new millennium. Paul was the first to go – a victim of his own hands – he put a gun to his head to take his own life, the etiology of which was clinical depression exacerbated by the consumption of alcohol. Eddie was next – he smoked himself to death – a victim of lung cancer caused by cigarette smoking. David was the next to go a victim of his own hands. David died of what I term a "drug- poisoning suicide." Basically his heart stopped as a result of a massive and lethal dose of smokeable cocaine. Melvin was the last to go resulting from chronic health issues he had been experiencing for years inclusive of chronic rheumatoid arthritis and finally succumbing to a brain seizure; from which he never regained consciousness, associated with heart failure. If you were born to be one of these Temptations – and I am convinced that you have to have been born to be a Temptation – your life expectancy would have been a meager forty-eight years from birth to death. And like Paul, Eddie, David and Melvin, Bernie Mac and Isaac Hayes, there are literally hundreds of other notable black men whose lives were cut short by disease and death.

They include men like Arthur Ashe age 50 (HIV/AIDS), James Baldwin age 63 (Cancer) Len Bias age 22 (Drug - Poisoning Suicide), James Brown age 72 (Congestive Heart Failure/Pneumonia), Sam Cooke age 33 (Homicide), John Coltrane age 41 (Liver Disease), Nat King Cole age 46 (Lung Cancer), Johnny Cochran age 60 (Brain Cancer), Miles Dewey Davis agie 65 (Stroke/Respiratory Failure/Pneumonia), Sammy Davis, Jr. age 65 (esophageal cancer), Medgar Evers age 38 (Homicide), Erroll Garner age 56 (Lung Cancer), Marvin Gaye age 45 (Homicide) Hank Gathers age 22 (Heart Disease), Donald Goines age 36 (Homicide), Dexter Gordon age 67 (Cancer), Fred Hampton age 21 (Legal Intervention/Homicide), Robin Harris age 39 (Heart Disease), Donny Hathaway age 33 (Suicide), Jimi Hendrix age 28

(Drug - Poisoning Suicide), Langston Hughes age 65 (Heart Disease), Bobby Hutton age 17 (Legal Intervention/Homicide), Michael Jackson age 50 (Drug Suicide) Martin Luther King age 39 (Homicide), Michael Jackson age 50 (Drug Suicide), George Jackson age 30 (Legal Intervention/Homicide), John Arthur (Jack) Johnson age 68 (Motor Vehicle Accident), Scott Joplin age 49 (Syphilis), Reggie Lewis age 27 (Heart Disease), Frankie Lymon age 26 (Drug -Poisoning Suicide), Reginald F. Lewis age 50 (Brain Cancer), Curtis Lee Mayfield age 57 (Diabetes and Paralysis Injuries), Lee Morgan age 34 (Homicide), Thelonious Monk age 65 (Stroke), Prince Rogers Nelson, age 55, (Drug Suicide), Huey P. Newton age 48 (Homicide), Adam Clayton Powell, Jr. age 64 (Prostate Cancer), Charlie "YardBird Parker age 35 (Heart Disease), Noel Pointer age 40 (Stroke), Richard Pryor age 65

(Cardiac Arrest), Otis Redding age 26 (Plane Cra

Ken Thompson, Brooklyn District Attorney, Reginald F. Lewis, Johnny Cochran, E, Steven Collins

sh), Jackie Robinson age 53 (Heart Disease), Max Robinson age 53 (HIV/AIDS), Don Rodgers age 23 (Drug-Poisoning Suicide), Al-Hajj Al-Malik Shabazz –Malcolm X age 39 (Homicide), Tupac Shakur age 25 (Homicide), Willie Smith age 39 (HIV/AIDS), Emmett Till age 14 (Homicide), Nat Turner age 31 (Lynching/Homicide), Luther Vandross, age 54 (Complication of Stroke), Christopher "Notorious Big" Wallace age 24 (Homicide), Mayor Harold Washington age 65 (Heart Disease), Dr. Amos Wilson age 53 (Stroke), Jackie Wilson age 52 (Stroke), Eric Eazy E Wright age 32 (HIV/AIDS), Richard Wright age 52 (Heart Disease), Barry White age 59 (Renal Failure) Whitney Young, Jr. age 50 (Drowning). And it happens to all too many of the most prominent, successful men who have ever walked among us.

Ken Thompson, the late District Attorney of Brooklyn, New York died of an aggressive form of colorectal cancer at age 50, shortly after taking office and after defeating the renowned long time Brooklyn District Attorney, Charles Hines. Reginald F. Lewis, financier, businessman, Wall Street magnet, and the first African American to build a billion dollar business; Beatrice International and author of "Why Should White Guys Have all The Fun,"died of brain cancer at age 50. Johnnie Cochran, a brilliant legal scholar and criminal trial lawyer died at age 67 of complications of a post op procedure to remove a cancerous brain tumor and E. Steve Collins a Philadelphia legendary journalist and radio personality; "The Voice aka "E," and Director of Urban Marketing for Radio One, civic leader and the host of "Philly Speaks," on Old school 100.3, died of a heart attack at age 58. Since his death E's wife has filed a lawsuit against Chestnut Hill hospital for medical negligence for the inappropriate emergency procedures that may have cost him his life. And while I'm not a conspiracy proponent I'd be inclined to believe that the same may be true for each of them; ????.

The above is but a small sample, an illustration of the pathological problem and etiology of excess and premature death of African American boys and men. Of these fifty-six (56) deaths documented herein; nearly all of them known to all of us, nearly thirty percent (29.6%) died before age (35) thirty-five. The average age at death was 44.6 years. Nearly fifty percent (48.1%) died before age (45) forty-five and more than fifty-five percent (55.5%) died before age (50) fifty. And only three of the fifty-four lived beyond age sixty-five (65) and only one, James Brown, lived to be 70 plus years of age. And nearly ninety-nine percent (98.1%) died before age (70) seventy. And believe it or not they represent the short list!

There is a haunting and horrific kind of sameness and consistency with respect to how the Boys of My Summers died and when. Doug Battle, a boy and a man who I loved immensely, died on June 8, 1981 at age 30 only twelve years after we graduated from high school. Doug died after having received a kidney transplant from his brother Terry. Terry"Mope" Battle, Doug's brother died twelve years later, in 1993, at age 42. Their brother Michael shared with me that Doug never left the hospital after the transplant and that for the next decade he and Terry "shot dope and destroyed Terry's remaining kidney. " The above obits and pictures are a profound

illustration of it's

backwardness and upside downness!!! Our lives were turned inside out, upside down, backwards, dying long before our parents, Eddie, Freddie, Gregory, Wayne, Toby.

Terry "Mope" Battle

Freddie Little died in 1988 at age 37 of a brain aneurysm. Gregory Jamison died in 1992 at 42 as a result of a drug overdose. Wayne Allen died in 1993 at 42 related to complications of a long term substance use disorder and pneumonia.

At Wayne's HomeGoing service a young negroidian peacher reminded us that; as he put it, "there are somethings that money can't buy." He went on to say that "money can buy people but it can't buy friends and it can't buy love, money can buy a house but it can't buy home, money and buy good doctors but it can't buy good health; and lastly he said, money can buy a beautyrest mattress but it can't buy a good night's sleep!"

Our mothers; all of them, of those of us dead or alive suffered to get a good night's sleep, now and along time ago.

Toby Scrivens (cause of death unknown to the writer) died at 41 and Charles Edward "Eddie" Franklin died in 1995 at age 45. Imagine this! More than fifty of the boys on this dead list died years before the guys I just named, years before. This is absolutely crazy! Who would have imagined, that this would have happened to us and how it would happen.

That each of these men has been deceased for for twenty-five years or more is a sad legacy. The longest being Doug, having been dead a little more than thirty-seven (37) years at the time of this writing. The next, Freddie has been dead for more than thirty (30) years. Gregory is third in line and has been dead more than twenty-six (26) years. Wayne, Terry and Toby have all been dead more than twenty-five (25) years and Eddie has been dead for twenty-three (23) years. The average age of death for this set of men was 39.6 years of age. Wow!!! Not only did they die young but they have also been gone; collectively, for more than a generation. Who could have predicted such a pandemic? Which of their mothers could have written such an epithet for any of them? I doubt seriously if any of them could have or would have. I knew their mothers and they would not have!

How is it that so many of us die so early in our life span? Why is our life span shorter than everyone else's? In the realm of life expectancy for all Americans – black women die before all women in America and black boys and men die before everybody!! What is it that we, African American boys and men, can do to take responsibility for saving our lives? How is it that we have grown so accustomed to our own dying that it almost seems normal to die at fifteen or twenty or thirty or forty years of age? How is it that as a people who have come up out of chattel slavery, Jim Crow-ism and the brutal system of lynching black people that occurred in America, that we seem to be and are now all too willing to lynch ourselves and to do so with impunity?

What is our dying about? What does it say of us? What will we do about it and when? What legacy will we leave? Why is it that in the greatest country in the history of the world that there exist these islands of third world health care within a continent of first world affluence? Why are we; in the 21st Century, still singing "We shall overcome someday?"

I may not have all of the answers to the questions I pose above but there is this that I know for sure. Unlike a plurality of the notable men aforementioned in this first chapter the Boys of My Summers "died not for a cause but because."

What I know for sure is that I need to add my voice to the conversation, share my insight and my passion for a willingness to save my own life, the life of my son and the lives of other boys and men who are willing to be saved. What I know for sure is that I am angry about what is and has been happening to us. And I refuse to allow anyone to tell me something is wrong with me because I am angry. See I read James Baldwin, an Ancestor, and I heard him when he said: "Find me a black man in America who is not angry and I'll show you a nigger who is in need of psychiatric help!" And I also refuse to have anyone tell me that I do not have the absolute right to save my own life! Black Lives have always and ought to always matter and it is up to us to act, behave and respond like we do!

What I know for sure, what I believe, is that we can stop this carnage by becoming "African American Men United to Save Our Lives."

And Then Michael Jackson Died:

The "King of Pop" Michael Jackson dies of an overdose of a prescription n drug or drugs; may be, at age 50 only weeks from celebrating a fifty-first birthday that was not to be. Another of the most talented, brilliant innovators of our time is gone. He was more than just an entertainer, but an American born, worldwide phenomena and popular culture, musical Icon. However, no matter how much money, fortune, talent or fame could keep Michael away from death's door.

Michael's demise is not unlike thousands of young black men who died as a result of; addiction to drugs, a drug induced overdose. In fact, Michael, with all due respect to his enormous contributions during his life and with respect to his family, his children especially, Michael is the last person in the line. Earl "Brother Moon" Thomas was a victim of an overdose of heroin in Trenton, New Jersey more than forty years ago. George "Kobo" Locket was also a casualty of a heroin overdose, in Trenton, New Jersey more than forty years ago. So was Milton Tucker, Jeffrey Goss, Karl Teape, Gregory Jamison, Elsie "El Sid" Smith, Melvin Smith, the twins Dale and David Fitzgerald. Dale and David were identical twins who died on the same day like they were born on the same day. They died together like they were born together. They died like they were born as twins and as brothers in the same place at the same time, their hearts stopping; one could presume, at the same time. All of them died of the same cause and they died before Michael, nearly all of them decades before him. Each of them was a boy of my summers, each of them a member of the short list representing those who died in the place where we all grew up.

Michael Jackson's death shook up our consciousness it shocked us and sent the world who loved him into mourning. This book is not about Michael Jackson but it could be because Michael, while like most of us, although I never met him in person it felt like I knew him, like I grew up with him. Michael was a child of my generation, a "baby boomer" born in the 1950's like many of the boys that I grew up with. Respecting and acknowledging the fact that I didn't personally know Michael and wanting to respect his memory I do want to speak to truth based on the information and accounts of Michael's death as learned by me through the same mechanisms, the media, the news, the statements from family and friends that we all heard. Any statements that are made herein with regard to Michael are based on the latter accounts. These statements are not meant to malign Michael's life or to character assassinate him or his family and friends.

However, it is to tell a particular kind of truth and to tell this truth from a place of knowing what it is to be addicted to opiate drugs. To tell the truth from a place of having been someone who knows the signs and symptoms of the disease of addiction and how it affects the lives of all of the people we are connected to even when they don't know they are being so affected. One of the most amazing things about Michael's death is how many of his family members and those who were his friends is how little many of them seemed to know about Michael's drug use and a chronic addiction to narcotic opiate type drugs. But from the place of knowing both as a recovering person and as a chemical dependency professional I also understand why this may have been the case. See, the disease of addiction gestates and grows inside of a protective cover or wall called denial. I know there is significant blame and responsibility being lane at the feet of the physician whose care Michael was under but if accounts about his long term drug use are true some of the blame for his death should be laid at Michael's feet and the long line of doctors who prescribed medication to him under a long list of aliases.

What is even more interesting is what is alleged to have happened, or should I say how Michael died. The difference in the boys who died as a result of a drug overdose and Michael's death is that he was, according to reports, being attended to by his doctor when he lost his life. Somebody was with him or supposed to be. Somebody was also with some the boys who I grew up with too. The problem is that in those cases they were not attended to by a physician but where either left in a hallway or stairwell like Brother Moon or dropped off at the entrance of the emergency room or they died alone in a basement, room or apartment.

Chapter Two:

"Trenton Makes, The World Takes"

A photo from The Trentonian

The boys and I grew up in Trenton, New Jersey were special guys in many respects. Back in the day we referred to Trenton as the "Big T." Although some of us were born in the earlier 1940's, most of us were born between 1945 and 1955. To give an illustration, Dan "Don" Roberson was born in 1946, Eugene "Wimp" Woodson was born in 1947, Charles "Slim" Oliver was born in 1948 and Gerald "Big Mug/Smash' McNiel was born in 1949.

(clockwise) Don, Wimp, Big Mug and Slim

The times that we grew up in were much less complex, simple - not better - depending on who you talk to - but certainly different. Trenton is a small city of approximately 85,000 inhabitants today. But I can remember when it was around 100,000 residents that populated our city. But it was a town where everybody knew everybody. The kids who you didn't know in elementary school you would meet at one of the five junior high schools. And if you didn't meet them at one of the junior high schools you would definitely meet them at Trenton Central High School. Everyone who went to high school when we were growing up, went to Trenton Central High School.

Trenton, New Jersey was a special place to grow up in. It is a place with a rich history connected to the birth of this country. It is the place where George Washington crossed the Delaware River from Pennsylvania to surprise the British/Hessian soldiers on Christmas Eve. Washington's crossing of the Delaware and the winning of the battle at Trenton that evening was a defining mark integral to the winning of the Revolutionary War and our country's subsequent independence.

Trenton, historically, is a blue collar town. It is the place where Winston Churchill Cigars were born and made. Yes, that Winston Churchill - the British-English Statesman and World War II, key player and hero.

TEEN TREAT BEATS
THE HEAT
KERNS RED
CREAM SODA
KERNS
CREAM SODA
KERNS
CREAM SODA
That's what it's all about. Kerns red cream soda is right on when you're hot, thirsty, or just want a special treat. And here's a pollution-solution tip . . . buy Kerns red cream soda in returnable bottles . . . it costs less — it's litter-less. Available almost everywhere.
E. L. KERNS COMPANY
TRENTON, NEW JERSEY

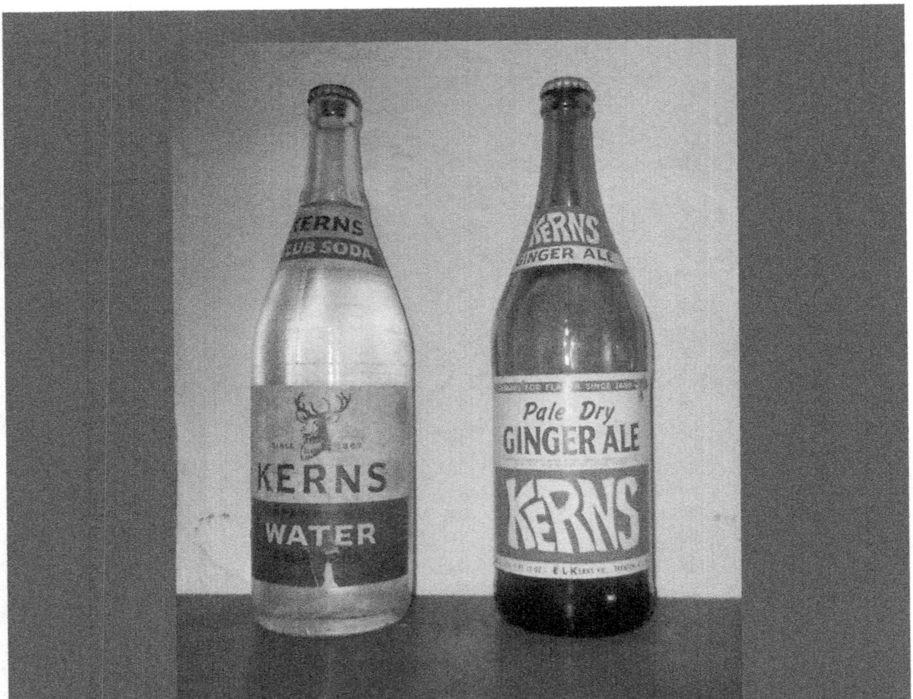

EL Kerns Club Soda, Quart, 1960 EL Kerns Ginger Ale, Quart 1972

Once upon a time, Trenton was a leading place of industry and manufacturing in the nation. Trenton industry manufactured everything from rubber, wire, rope, ceramics, cigars and much, much more. Trenton was the home of the Champale Bottling Co. (Beer), Borden's Milk Company, The Kerns Bottling Co. (Soda), Gould Battery Co., CV Hills Air Conditioning and Refrigeration, Demag DeLaval (Turbomachinery), Acme Rubber, General Motors, Horsman Doll Company, Young's Rubber Co. (the maker of Trojans condoms), John A. Roebling & Sons (Steel Company), The Pittsburgh Glass Company, American Standard, Trenton Old Stock Beer and the Lee Jean Company; that's right – the Lee Jean Company – just to name a few. There was not a better tasting

Cream Soda on the planet than the Red Cream they made and bottled at Kerns. I'm sure that there are folks who would disagree with me and would vote for the orange or grape but for this professional soda taster, it was the Cream without a doubt!

R.C. Maxwell Co. Trenton N.J.
Trenton
OLD STOCK
BEER
PEOPLES BREWING COMPANY

Trenton
Beer

Trenton
Old Stock
BEER

Trenton
Old Stock
BEER

HOME OF
Trenton
OLD STOCK
BEER

Champale and Grenadine

Trenton is the home of the first professional basketball game and it has produced some of the nation's best sport athletes including Al Downing who played for the New York Yankees, Oakland Athletics, Milwaukee Brewers and the Los Angeles Dodgers from 1961-1977. Al's greatest claim to fame; ironically, is that he pitched the home run ball to Hank Aaron, the pitch and the hit, heard around the world, that broke Babe Ruth's all time homerun record at 715. Trenton is the place that gave birth to Elvin Bethea, inducted into the Professional Football Hall of Fame in 2003 and Defensive End for the NFL's Houston Oilers/Tennessee Titans and a graduate of North Carolina A&T University and was the first person and player inducted into the hall of fame from that school and his grand high school almatur, Trenton Central High School, respectively. And unbeknownst to many it is the city where the first professional Basketball game was played. And one of the best high school basketball players to ever play the game and not to ever to play in the NBA, Nate "The Great" Armstrong.

David Dinkins

Trenton is also the hometown and birthplace of the man who would become the first African American Mayor of the town that has been deemed the crossroad of the world; New York, New York, a town "so nice they had to name it twice." David Dinkins epitomizes the richness and the greatness of Trentonians and lends itself to the illuminating legacy that springs from and shines through the night from a bridge that exclaims, "Trenton Makes The World Takes!"

My own claim to some fame is that before our homeboy became the Mayor of New York, he was the Manhattan Borough President. There was a day when I was summoned by my boss, Elizabeth Gaynes of the Osborne Association to be present at a meeting at the Borough President's office. I was taken aback, awed and almost astonished when I arrived to find that I had a seat at a table with the host of the meeting, Borough President David Dinkins, across the table from me was; at that time, the New York State's Special Narcotics Prosecutor, Sterling Johnson, to his left was the renowned and longtime District Attorney of Manhattan the Honorable Robert Morgenthau, to my right sat another renowned District Attorney of the County of Kings, the borough of Brooklyn, the Honorable, Mr. Charles Hines and to my left sat the first African American District Attorney of the Bronx, New York, the Honorable Mr. Robert Johnson and seated at the far end of the table was one of the historical innovators of drug treatment in New York City, the Honorable, Mr. Sidney Mochett, at that time the Executive Director of Reality House, Inc., an institution located on the far west end of the historic 125th Street in Harlem.

Here I was, a little cat from Trenton, sitting down stream from a homeboy whose father had a barbershop and a real estate company on Spring Street who years before I'd hired to take care of the affairs of the home I'd left behind as a rental property when I moved to New York, a homeboy who would become the Mayor of the crossroad of the World. It's a small world, indeed.

Unbeknownst to many Dennis Rodman of Chicago Bulls, Detroit Pistons and San Antonio Spurs basketball fame is a native

Trentonian. One of the greatest jazz trumpeters that most of us never knew we heard, was Johnny Coles, aka "Little Johnny C" was also a Trenton native. Johnny Coles played with some of the jazz greats including the Duke Ellington and Gil Evans bands and with Charles Mingus and the Herbie Hancock quintet. His trumpet play was like that of one of the best, Miles Dewey Davis.

Al Downing

Elvin Bethea

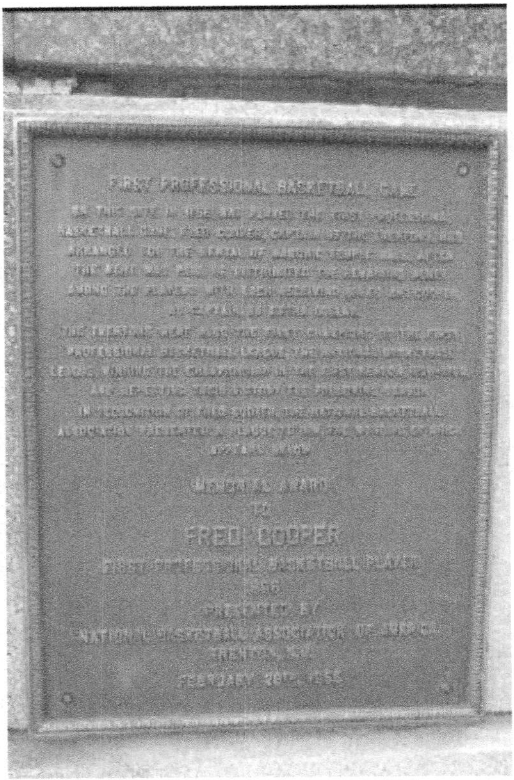

Plaque of the first Professional Basketball Game played in Trenton

Trenton was also a mecca of boxing. Although many of the fighters who turned pro fought out of Philadelphia, Trenton was the place where they honed their skills. These boxers include the late great Ike Williams who won and owned the lightweight championship of the world from 1945 - 1951. There were many greats from Trenton like George Johnson (60-22-0-31K0's). JD Ellis was a very good boxer who was a pro and who worked with young and upcoming boxers at the P.A.L Gym at the Stadium Pool Complex on Reservoir Street.Then there was a legendary Sammy Goss, Trenton's own 1968 Olympian at Mexico City. As far as Trenton boxing goes Sammy was a legend in his own time, especially as an amatuer. The boys of my summers in the world of amateur boxing included the names Lindsey "Butch/Monster"Page, David "Poppy"Sanderson, John Paul Lacy, Muhammad "Red" Berry, John "Denny" Glover, Obie English, John "Pie" Hodges, Lance Hodges, Don Roberson, Harold Carroll, Rufus Watkins, Tyrone Johnson, Hedgepeth, Lewis Payton, Harold Carol, Sylvester Livingston, Regis "Azim" Gates, Lee Grant Moses, Ricky Hightower, John Deal, Jody White and the beloved James "Crazy Jack" Thomas, most of who trained under the watchful eye of the legendary professional cut man, the late Honorable Percy Richardson.

One of the best fights ever in the history of the AAU Golden Gloves Championships was at 106 lbs., between the reigning champ, a dude by the name of Elijah Cooper and Trenton's own David "Poppy" Sanderson. Elijah Cooper was a bad boy, no question about it and everyone knew it. However I felt and knew the same about "Poppy," he could fight too and I was betting money and took odds that he would win. There was almost nobody except me, in our section, all Trenton folks, who believed that Poppy stood a chance. In fact they compared his chances of winning to that of a "snowball freezing over in hell!" Yet during and after the 1st Round ended I heard some "damn's" and some "damn's I didn't know that Poppy could fight."

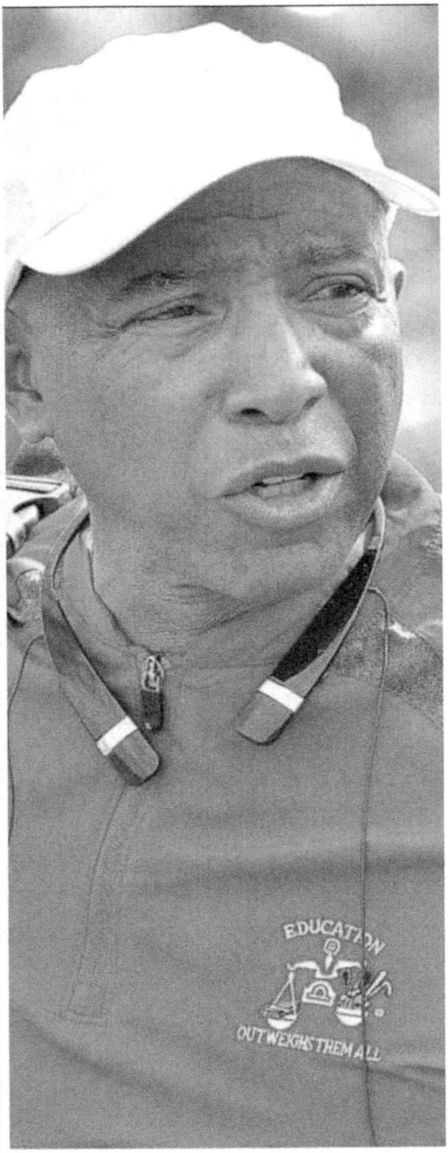

By the end of the 2nd Round they all knew that Poppy could fight and that he may have outfought Cooper. By the end of the 3rd

Round, I was jumping up and down, screaming at the top of lungs, "I told you so, I told you so!" As we waited for the decision I was still hollering when the raised Cooper's arm as the winner. And while I lost money that night the vindication that I felt was exhilarating and in fact I believe that Poppy won the fight and while they didn't give me my money back, a bunch of them believed like I did Poppy won the fight. I raised some much hell about the decision that they threatened to put me out of the building.

Another of the great fights were between Sammy Goss and Lewis Payton. Lewis was trained by Mr. Leggett Sr. (Bucky's father) in a small gym on Wayne Avenue. The Goss/Payton fight were in my mind one of the greatest amatuer classics in Trenton's boxing history and although Sammy was the victor; with all due respect, while some will vehemently and ardently disagree I am convinced that in one of their fights Payton edged Sammy by decision. It was the same for me with Sammy Goss vs. John Paul Lacy. John Paul was younger but he was a gym rat who could fight. He was both sharp, smart and sweat. Unfortunately, he fought in the same weight class as Sammy at 126 pounds and would meet him in the final Golden Glove bout two straight years and again both fights were no blow outs for Sammy, John Paul held his own and my boxing eye and maybe my heart too, said that John Paul edged Sammy out in their last fight. I took odds and betted with John Paul and lost money. However, we'd argue for a few weeks about who won the fight. The boxing season started in Elizabeth, New Jersey and woul end with the finals in Trenton, first at Moose Hall and later at the Civic Center. If you were there you got to see the likes of. Ernest Best and Levi Sessions, Newark Duker boys, Gypsy Joe Harris. Bobby "Boogaloo" Watts, "Straight Outta Philly" and our homeboy James "Crazy Jack" Thomas. Glorious days they were.

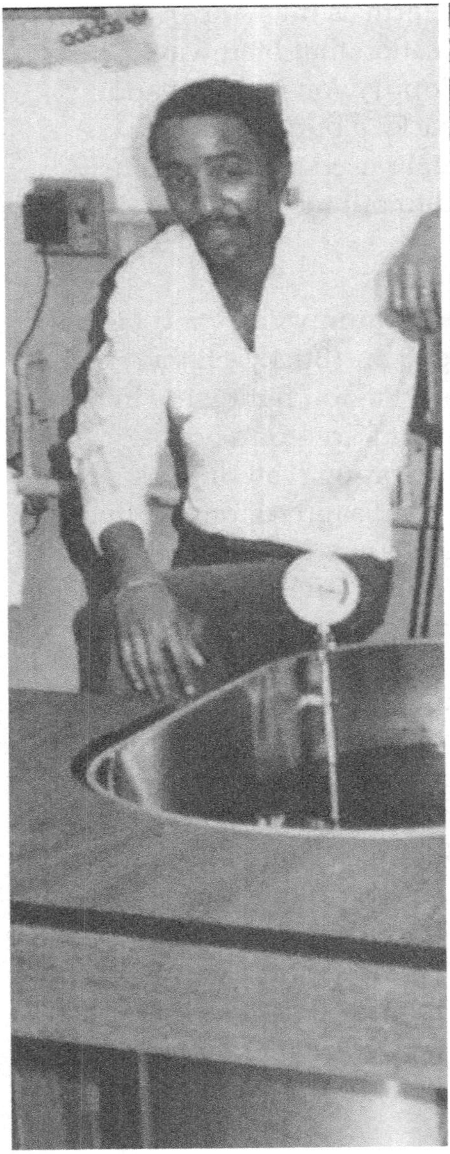

One of the very best middleweights that most of us didn't get to see was James "Jimmy" Nunley. Should he have chosen a different path there are those who knew him who were convinced that he would have been a middleweight contender. I was privileged to see him in action; not in the ring but in the streets of Harlem, when he was at his physical worse, I watched him knock out a big muscled dude that I'd known as an acquaintance from jail. It actually was one of the most vicious knockouts I'd seen, bar none!

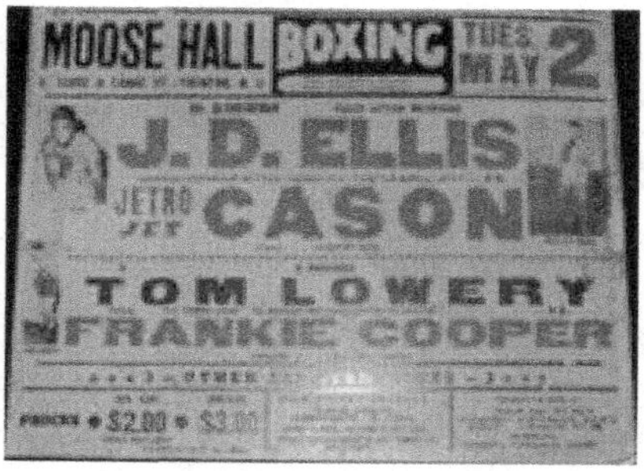

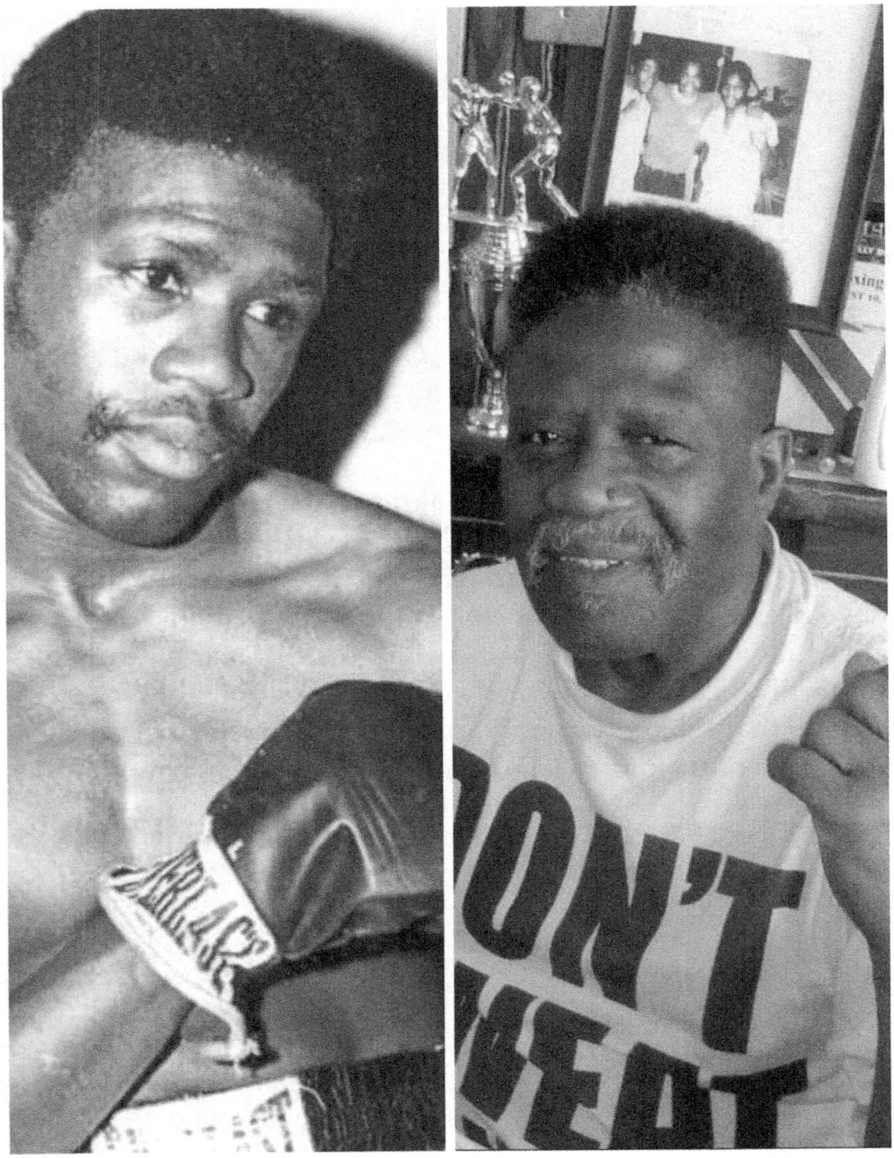

Sammy Goss

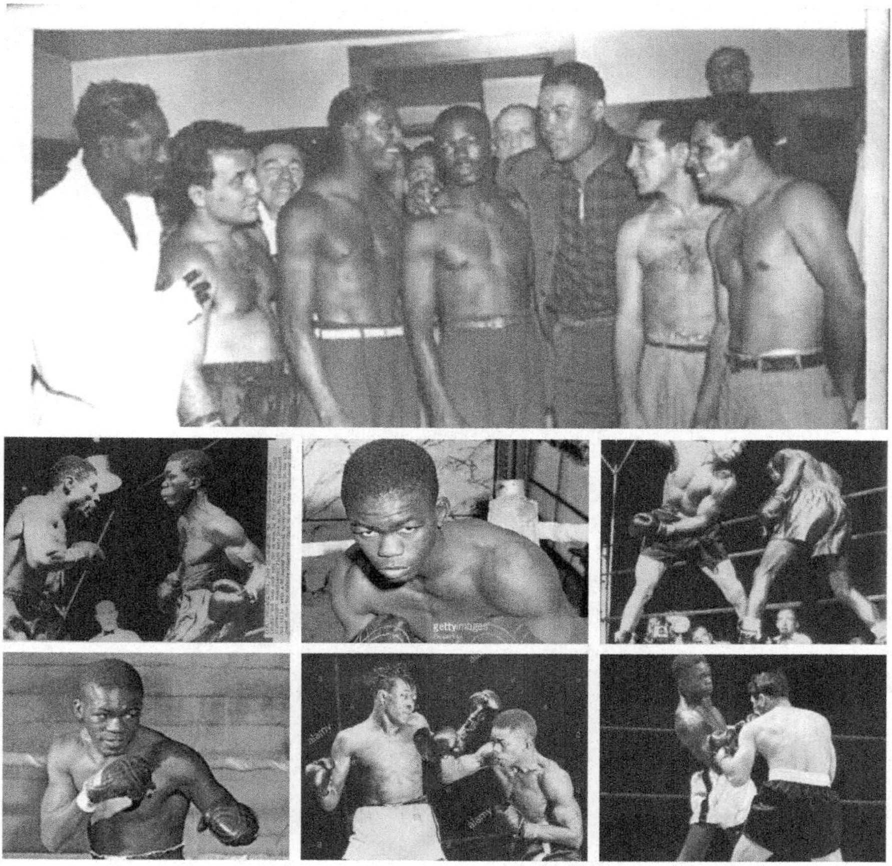

Ike Williams (Lightweight Champion of the World April 18, 1945 - May 25, 1951)

One of the most superb boxers of his time he fought in one of the most corrupt periods in boxing history was Trenton's own Ike Williams. He was also a cousin/uncle of mine who, like my parents, came to Trenton, from Georgia, in the era of the "Great Negro Migration" from the agricultural south to the industrial north.

Trentonian Photo By Vince Gianformesi

CYO BOXING ACTION — There were plenty of action-packed bouts on the recent pro fight card held at the CYO Center in Trenton. In one of the bouts (top photo) Trenton's Lindsey Page used some powerful right hand shots to score a unanimous decision over Curtis Pitman of New York City. Trenton lightweight Benny DeJesus (right, bottom photo) also landed some solid rights on Paul Moore of Philadelphia. Moore, however, came away with a decision in the bout. Pro boxing action returns to the CYO Center on S. Broad Street in January.

Butch "Monster" Page

There were other cats who could fight and their fights were in the street and some of the were some of the hardest punchers to come through our universe. Dudes like Charles Boston, better known as "Tex" whose reputation was that when locked up in Jamesburg he put a cow on its knees with a punch. I was able to see his punch in action when he knocked out one of my childhood friends. A group of us walked over to Summer Street to watch our friend Tyron Johnson; a hard young boy puncher's himself, fight a boy named Theodore. When Theodore saw us he called out, "hey Butch." Butch turned out to be Tex, who responded by walking up to Tyrone and with what seemed like the flick of his wrist and a tap on Tyrone's jaw,sent him to his knees, crawling through Tex's legs and flipping over on his side, it was amazing to watch it happen and the legend became real, especially for Tyrone. Then there Burley Saunders, a Mike Tyson tank of a manchild who could knock you out with either hand. Tex and Burley where Trenton Mikes Tyson's before Mike Tyson. There were dudes like Dan Livingston, Ervin "BaBro" Davis, Jimmy Davis, Jerry Daniels, Lee Fuller, Willie "Blue Chip"Davis, Jesse Lee Harris, Bunky Glover and two other hard punchers, Bobby Rutherford and Stan Derry and a little cat by stature named Larry Bostick and a host of others.

Trenton used to be a place of commerce and industry but it was also a great place to grow up. Trenton, a small/mid-size city, was when I and the children I grew up with could expect one of the finest public school educations in the country. When I say the finest, I mean the best - the best schools and the best teachers, a scholastic experience that was *second to none.*

As aforementioned most of the "Boys of My Summers" were born between 1945 and 1955, some were born a few years earlier but most of them were born within this ten year age group. The oldest of us if they had lived would have been nearly seventy; most though not yet ready to retire before they died, at least not at age sixty-five. The youngest of us lost to this early demise would have been nearly sixty-three. We are baby boomers who grew up in a simple, challenging, difficult, historic and wonderful time to be born in America and especially in Trenton.

Growing up in Trenton was kind of like living both in the city and in the country. We grew up in neighborhoods, blocks and on streets where the "four o'clock;" a flower, was the flower you had to have on your small front lawn – if you had a front lawn. We lived on streets called Sweets Avenue, Fountain Avenue, Division Street, Hart Street, Lamberton Street, Old Rose Street, New Rose Street, Union Street, New Willow Street, Wilson Street, Brunswick Avenue, Passaic Street, Hanover Street, Wayne Avenue, Southard Street, Clinton Avenue, Walnut Avenue, South Cook Avenue, Lincoln Avenue, Greenwood Avenue, East and West State Street, Stuyvesant Avenue, Parkside Avenue, Locust Street, South Broad Street, Burton Avenue, Oliver Avenue, Hermitage Avenue, Chambers Street, Humboldt Street, Reservoir Street, Spring Street, Kelsey Avenue, Calhoun Street, Dell Street, Botanique Street, Dunham Street. We grew up in a time where public housing – like Prospect Village, The Campbell Homes ("Frazier Homes – as most of us it called it), The Donnelly Homes, The Lincoln Homes were places where grass grew and children were forewarned to keep off the grass. We were all alive when the Miller Homes not the "Killer Homes" was built.

Recognize: "This Is How We 'Still' Do It!"

In Loving Memory Of

James Tyrone Kelly

Sunrise: January 01, 1950

Sunset: September 26, 2017

Muslim Cemetery of South Florida

September 30th 2017

On the street where I lived – Dunham Street – located in Northwest Trenton, off Calhoun Street – one of our favorite past times was to trap bumble bees – "yellow jackets" – praying mantis', butterflies and grasshoppers. We would catch them in glass jars with metal tops with holes punch through so that these creatures could get air. We would watch joyfully as the praying mantis would devour a grasshopper head first. We were young scientist studying the world of insect behavior. We'd catch ants – the big black ones and gently drop them onto the bed of a spider's web.

We'd anxiously await the spider coming from her or his den to see what the disturbance was about. We would watch as she claimed her prize and wrap it up for safekeeping and return to her den. We would also drop the big red headed stick matches into the hole of the trunk of a big tree in my backyard and watch the big black ants furiously bring them out and rest them at the base of the tree. We, Dorsey and I, would also pay the consequences of such conduct when Mr. David, Dorsey's father, caught us burning out the ants and burned up our behinds with the blazing swings and strokes of his belt. He had to climb over a fence between my backyard and theirs but we were so busy we didn't see him coming. And even if we had we couldn't have gotten away. Back then father's where still home and even somebody else's could whip your behind, and they could run!

By the way, when we were growing up it was permissible for adults, who had good sense, to whip your behind, your parents or anybody else's, anytime and at any place. See, back then or "back in the day" everybody knew everybody else's children. They, "grown – ups," knew who your parents were and they knew where you lived, who your brothers and sisters where or if you were like me they knew you didn't have any. They knew if you were a "latch key" kid. They knew if you were home alone. They knew if your parents worked or not and when they would be home from work. Oftentimes punishment for childish transgressions would have been exacted and executed - they felt like near executions at the time they were happening - before your parents got home. And if you were fortunate you didn't get another "beating" by your parents just on the (GP) general principles of the era.

It was even permissible for teachers to exact corporal punishment if they thought it fit the behavior, prank or disturbance to classroom equilibrium, normalcy or ethics. And it seemed that all of them would at one time or another, especially in elementary school and as well in junior high school. One of the most vivid of these memories is the time that Mr. Copeland; Mr. Cosby Copeland, who was a physical education teacher at Jr.1, cleared the locker room and dug into the behind (ass) of one young Mr. Bradley Boyd who had recently returned home and back to school from Jamesburg Youth Reformatory. Bradley was being disrespectful and Mr. Copeland who would years later become the Superintendent of Trenton's school system, was also a former "semi-pro" football player for the Newark Bears, was having none of it! Mr. Copeland looked like and was the size of Mike Singletary, Hall of Fame Linebacker for the Chicago Bears and when he hit you, ran into you, tackled you, it was with grown man force and Bradley paid a dear price that day and those of us who could hear it and those of us who peered over or around the lockers to see it; which was also dangerous, learned a valuable lesson that day, "do not "fuck" with Mr. Copeland!!! And his partners, Mr. Page, Mr. Dudack and Mr. Dunn (Red) would also tear your ass up!! And if you didn't know and didn't ask somebody and you sold a "wolf ticket" to Mr. Taylor you were subject to wake up on your back. Mr. Taylor was about 5'6" tall however, he was one of those men and teachers that it wasn't about the "size of the dog in the fight, it's about the size of the fight in the dog!

Mr, Taylor

At Jr.1, gym class was like a mini boot camp. When the bell rang and the next class was gym class you had to run to the locker room from whichever floor you were on and the locker room was in the basement of the building. We would have 5 minutes to strip naked and change into joke strap, gym uniform, shirt and shorts, sweat socks and sneakers and be standing at attention in your particular squad line and if you were a squad leader like I was, when called on you had to announce that your squad was "all present and accounted for, all prepared!!" The fastest boy in our class to do the five minute transition was David "Poppy" Sanderson and he would do it in under 5 minutes and he did it in all three years we were there.

Gym class at Jr.1 was like being in the United State Marine Corps or the United States Army, seriously! We were required to climb ropes that ascended almost to the gym's ceiling. We had to run a mile which comprised five laps around a gravel track, we did jumping jacks, push ups, pull ups and situps. I remember heavy boys, aka fat boys, straining, sweating, trembling sometimes even crying in the struggle to get less than a quarter of the way up the rope. I remember our class running the mile; there was a huge tree on the other side of the track by Jefferson Elementary School, Earl Taylor and Charles Thomas decided that they would hide behind the tree and join up with us on the last lap. Problem was that unbeknownst to them they'd been spotted when they first ducked behind the tree; a shanegin that had been tried for years, and the price for doing so meant that when the lap ended they were told to keep running and it meant that they would continue to run for the rest of the school day, lap after lap. It also worked as a deterrent for the rest of us throughout our tenure at Jr.1 and it became household folklore throughout the school.

And no matter what school you attended all of us had a story to tell about a teacher or teachers who ruled their respective classrooms with an iron fist. In my elementary school; Monument, Mr. Cox; foremost among them, Ms. Manning, Ms. Rotonda, Mr. Ham, Ms. Newsome, and Ms. Woodson were some of them. In Jr.1 it was Mr. Coordery, Mr. Moskovic who were both crazy. And guess what? Our parents loved it, they embraced it and gave their blessing. If you had to go to the principal's office or you were looking straight into your parents eyes the message was always clear and always the same - you were in school to learn, to get an education.

My mother would talk to me when she whipped me, which in my case was fairly often. And Bernice could whip some behind! I was just one of those kids who you might say was a handful. But Bernice would almost sing when she whipped me. Her cadence and rhythm were consistent with her "boy didn't I tell you not to....."
It seemed as if what we called "beatings" would last forever but they never seemed to deter me from working on getting another one - I'd get into something every day, almost. And Bernice would, again indulge in one of her favorite pastimes - singing.

But in spite of this it was a wonderful time to grow in and Trenton was a wonderful city to grow up in and our schools were wonderful places to learn and our teachers who were also our coaches, were the very, very best that any child could have been taught by.

Trenton; when we were growing up, was a wonderful town filled with traditions, especially the parades. The parades on

Thanksgiving, Labor Day and the Fourth of July were events to look forward to and the highlight of every parade was the anticipation, the tapping on the ground, the footsteps, the black shining boots hitting the black top and the growing roar of the crowd parade. You'd hear them before you could see them but you were absolutely certain that within minutes you were about to witness a home grown phenomena, the great Cavaliers Drill Team, led by Mr. Bingham who himself was a living legend. It is only a Trentonian of this era who can enjoy the historical sentiments expressed herein about the Cavaliers. The Cavaliers were an award winning precision drill team that embodied the best of Trenton's sons. They were and looked fantastic wearing their classic red and white Cavalier hats with the long red or white ostrich feathers, white satin bloused shirts and red pants with the white stripe and the shining black, white laced boots. And man, could they drill. Even today, I doubt that there is a drill team in the country that could compete with what they did and how they did it back then. And in fact the Cavaliers are an institution that endures to this day with some of its members in their fifties and sixties still drilling.

Mr. Bingham and the Cavaliers

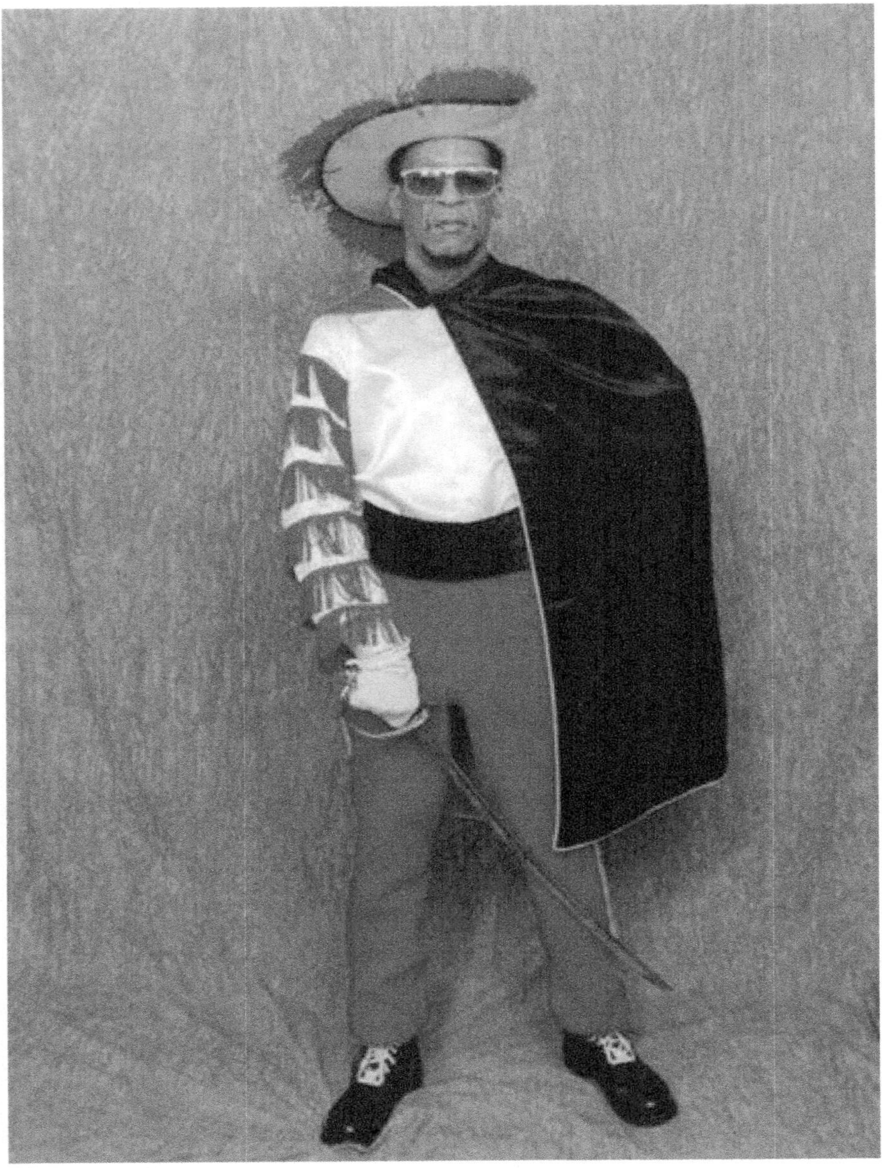

I never knew where the parades began. But what I did know is that they always came through the intersections of Broad Street, Brunswick Avenue, Princeton Avenue, Pennington Avenue and Warren Streets at The Battle Monument Park and at the historic "Five Points." The parade would cross Pennington Avenue on to Warren Street and would continue down Warren all the way to Stacy Park, where the parade would end.

However, the cascade of the death knell did not and sadly has not escaped members of one of Trenton's greatest prides, the Cavaliers. The members of the team make up (7.5%), nearly eight percent of the boys on the list of those who this book is written in remembrance of and to celebrate their living. They include Charlie, Wayne, Robert "Junie Babe" Bethea; one of the clusters of brothers represented in this book, Elsie "El Sid" Smith, David Hill, Ronnie Denson, Leroy King, James "Denny" Jones, Jesse Logan, Charles "JB" Haywood, Charles Coley, Charles Belcher, Felix "Monk" Slaughter, Joe Thorpe, Jody Williams, Scotty Miller, Alton Grier and Carl McCall, to name a few.

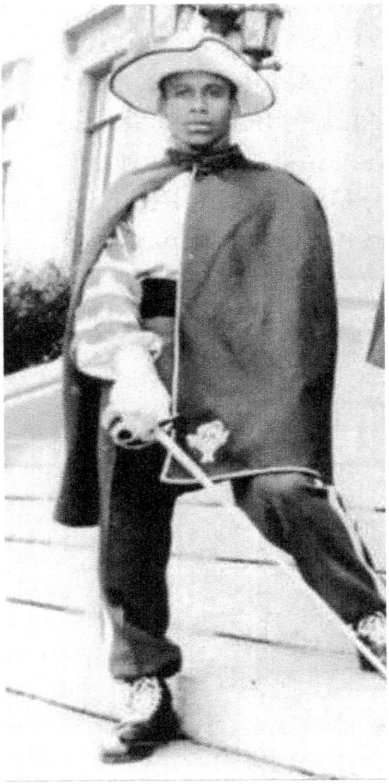

Junie Babe

Homegoing Celebration
For Our Beloved
Steven S. Miller
Sunrise
August 22, 1951
Sunset
April 11, 2017

Scotty

CAVALIERS
DRILL
TEAM
TRENTON, N.J.

The Cavaliers: David "Poppy" Sanderson, Lewis Matlock

El Sid (Elsie Smith)

Halloween was also a great Trenton tradition for both children and their parents. It was great fun from school to the night of Trick or Treat. It was safe and supervised. We would walk for miles to get candy. The kids from Dunham and Wilson Street and Pashley Avenue would walk all the way to Ewing Township, which was a predominately white enclave but they had the best candy. In fact it was in the home of one of these families in Ewing that I and my friends saw our first color television. Like Catherine Ellison, a lifelong girl friend and sister of "Slim Jenkins" we both remember distinctly that it was Bonanza, the Cartwright's - Ben, the father, Little Joe, Hoss, and Adam, in living color in the living room of white people who had welcomed us into the their home and we left with great candy.

If you grew up with us in the 1950's and 1960's, you lived in Trenton and you had twenty cents you could eat one of the best hot dogs in the world at Kresge's Five and Ten located at the corner of State and Broad Streets. The hot dogs were fifteen cents and a small-big glass of root beer cost a nickel. Down the street or around the corner on Broad Street was the Capital movie theater and to the east of State Street was the Mayflower movie theater and to the west on Warren Street was the Trent movie theater. But the best movie was uptown at the Five Points – the RiAlto Movie Theater, aka "The Ranch." The RiAlto cost a quarter to get in and the treat was two movies, a cartoon in between and a candy lolly pop that was the size of your head and only cost a nickel. We were movie kids who went to the movie on Sunday's and we saw everything that came out.

We grew up on classic movies like the three hour long epic Ben Hur and the Ten Commandments, starring Charlton Heston, Spartacus, starring Kirk Douglas, Tarzan The Ape Man starring Gordon Scott, Hercules Unchained starring Steve Reeves, Yul Brynner in Taurus Bulba, West Side Story, Samson and Delilah starring Victor Mature, Davy Crockett starring Vest Parker, The Disney Classics, Darby O'Gill and The Little People, The Tales of Sleepy Hollow, Snow White and the Seven Dwarfs, horror films like the Night of The Living Dead, Frankenstein, The WolfMan and The Teenage WereWolf. We'd seen all of the movies before we were sixteen years old.

We grew up in a television era that included weekly series like the Rifleman starring Chuck Connors, Wanted Dead or Alive starring Steve McQueen, Cheyenne starring Clint Walker, Wagon Train starring Ward Bond. There were others like the Donna Reed Show, Leave it to Beaver, My Three Sons starring Fred MacMurray, Bat

Masterson starring Gene Barry, Maverick starring James Garner, Father Knows Best starring Robert Young, American Bandstand hosted by Dick Clark, The Ed Sullivan Show, The Andy Griffin Show, I Love Lucy, M Squad starring Lee Marvin, Dragnet, Seventy Seven Sunset Strip starring Evelyn Symbliss Jr., Hawaiian Eye, The Real McCoy's starring Walter Brennan, The Beverly Hillbillies and Barnaby Jones, The Mod Squad, The Andy Williams Show, Perry Como Show and The Flip Wilson Show and The Ed Sullivan Show, Search For Tomorrow, The Days of Our Lives, One Life To Live, All My Children, General Hospital and Dark Shadows.

Then there was the Lit Brothers Department Store on Broad Street near the Capital, Dunham's Department Store on Broad Street, Woolworth's, Robert Hall's, Nevius and Voorhees and the famous Lee Jean Company on East State Street and Sears and Roebuck on Stockton Street, Littman's Jewelers, Havenson's, Simon's, Charlie Byers', The Shirt Shop all lined Broad Street between State and Perry Streets and Rauches' Coats on East Hanover Street. And uptown at the Five Points was Sam's Hat Shop. The best and most fashionable clothes money could buy. And if you lived in North Trenton and you bought Stevie Wonder's "Fingertips" 45 record more likely than not you bought it from a historical institution that has stood on the former Princeton Avenue, renamed Martin Luther King Boulevard called the "ACE RECORD SHOP." The photo of the ACE RECORD SHOP is one of the last remaining and surviving relics of a time long past, of the way we were, the 5 Points, of Trenton and what ought to be a historical landmark.

Trenton was a wonderful place to grow up in with wonderful schools and great institution like the Carver Center YMCA on Fowler Street another and still living and historical landmark. The Boys of My Summers and I grew up in some of the most tranquil and turbulent times in our nation's history in general and the City of Trenton, New Jersey in particular.

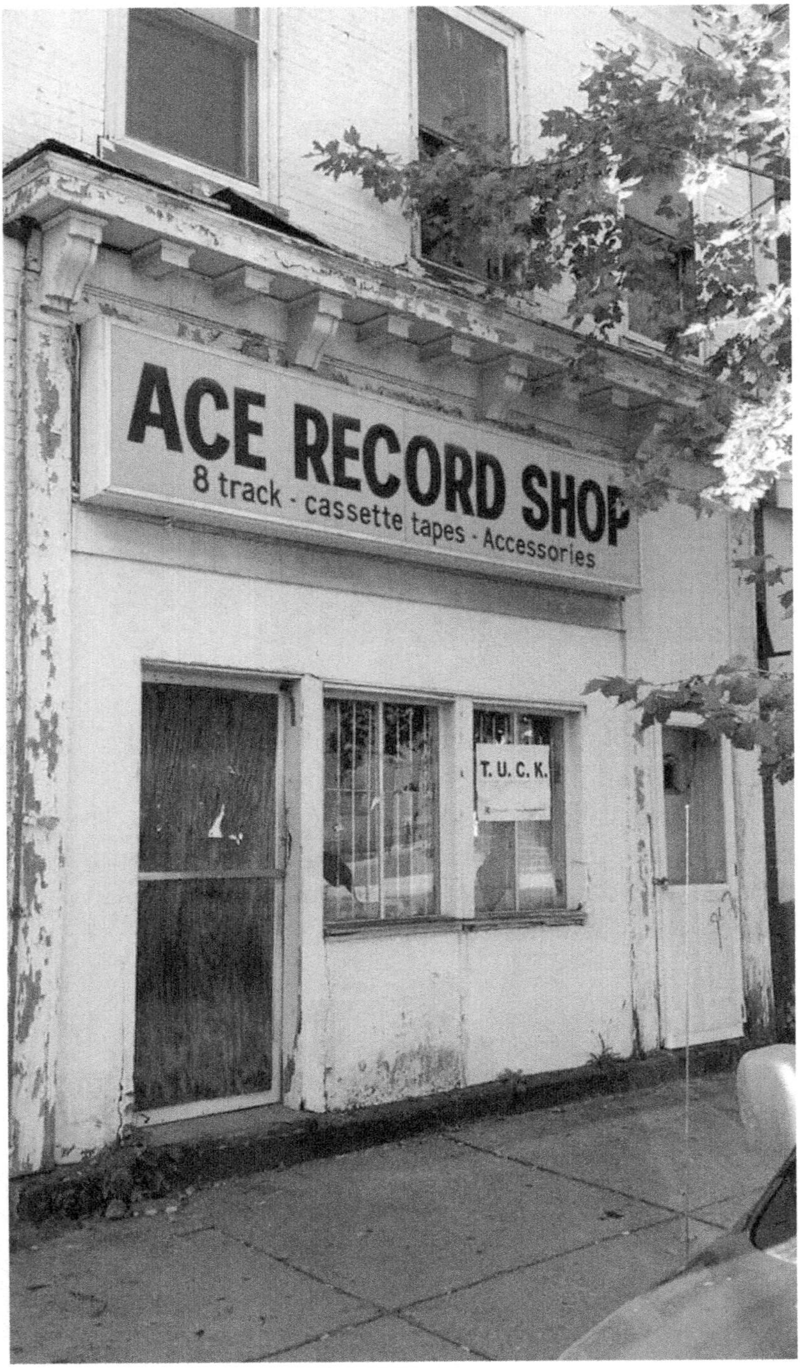
ACE RECORD SHOP
8 track - cassette tapes - Accessories
T. U. C. K.

While writing this book another of the Boys passed. His name was Henry "Bro" Ellison, Jr., aka "Slim Jenkins." He was one of the closes of my childhood friends. There was a time in our growing up when we were inseparable. My friend died on Sunday, August 15, 2009 shortly after celebrating his fifty-ninth birthday on June 30, 2009. He was a man who I'd known for fifty-five years.

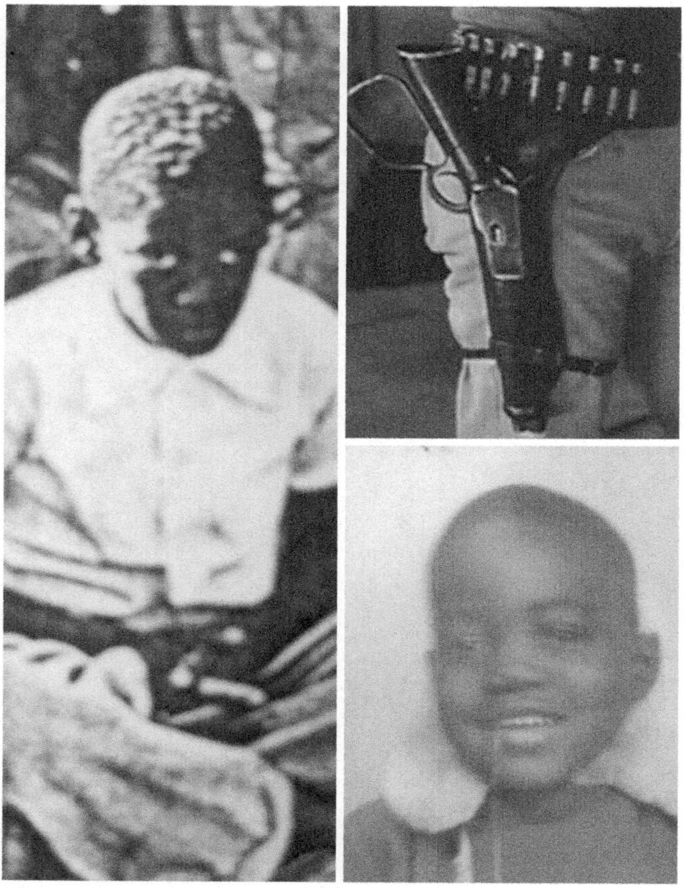

Bro aka "Slim Jenkins" and Me

We had known one another nearly all of our lives. In fact it could have been even longer because the truth be told I really can't remember when I didn't know him.

Celebration of Life

For

Henry Ellison, Jr.

"Slim Jenkins"

Sunrise
June 30, 1950

Sunset
August 16, 2009

Services:

Monday, August 24, 2009

1:00 p.m.

Campbell Funeral Chapel

1225 Calhoun St., Trenton, New Jersey 08608

Rev. Pamela Taylor

Officiating

He died a little more than nine years ago. He was a boy who I skipped rocks with across the creek, went swimming with in the muddy pond we found in Pennsylvania, across the Calhoun Street Morrisville Bridge. We shoveled snow off the black topped basketball court at the Monument School playground. He taught me how to pick blueberries and tomatoes when we went to the "farm" during the summer months. We had two puppies from the same litter his puppy was named "Fluffy" and my puppy was named "Tippy." The puppies came from "Sally's" litter. Sally was owned by the Wade family who lived on Wilson Street right around the corner from Dunham Street where we lived. His puppy was slim or skinny and my puppy was chubby or fat which was pretty much how we were, he was tall and skinny and I was short and chubby and it stayed that way for the rest of our lives.

When we were nine years old and in the fourth grade Steve McQueen was starring in the aforementioned TV series "Wanted Dead or Alive." He was a fast drawing, fast shooting cowboy who we loved. His claim to fame though and the thing that made him different from any of the other cowboys was the gun he carried and the holster that held it. The gun was a sawed off Winchester rifle (pictured above) looking gun, held in a swivel like holster that allowed him not to have to draw the gun but just to swing it upward and shoot from his hip. God, this was a bad gun and a toy replica of it was being sold that Christmas season of 1959. After school one afternoon we decided to go downtown. Downtown Trenton back then was the epicenter of shopping back in the day. We had no money and by all intent and purpose we should not have been downtown.

We were two little black boys without our parents who decided to go into Lit Brothers Department Store and there it was, the toy gun replica carried by Steve McQueen. Immediately, I had to have one. My parents would have bought me one for Christmas if I'd have put it in as a present I wanted, they always did. But I couldn't wait. The lure of this gun was so tantalizing that I had to have it now and Bro was with me. I don't think he agreed with my taking it but because he was with me he came along for the ride so to speak. We were on our way down the escalator and I had the gun under my coat.

When we got to the bottom a white man who had been riding behind us placed his hand on both of our shoulders and directed us to a room at the back of the store. I'd been caught and because I'd been caught Bro was caught with me. The man was a "store detective" called "Loss Prevention" these days, and while we were in the office he opened up a drawer where there was a gun that appeared to be a real one. Then he told both of us to stand with our backs against a wall and seemingly he measured us for our height. He then proceeded to ask us our names, where we lived, our parents name and their home phone numbers. We cooperated and gave him everything. After about a half hour we were let go and were told that our parents would be called. When we got out of the store it was dark and we were lost or should I say a little disoriented as we had never been downtown at night, not by ourselves. We finally got our bearings by locating the top of the Battle Monument which is at the Five Points and used it as our guide. Once we got to the Five Points we were in familiar territory and it was smooth sailing home.

However, I was scared to death about the phone call the man said he was going to make. Although it was dark it was only about 5 o'clock in the evening and my mother had not yet gotten home from work. I got in the house and sat by the phone hoping that the man would call and I was prepared to do an Oscar winning performance as I was going to star as my mom because if I was not successful and the man talked to the real mom, Bernice, my life come to an abrupt end, of that I was sure. As it turned out the man never called. But the fact that he didn't served to have me be a nervous wreck for about two weeks still sitting by the phone ready to play Bernice. My mother would have killed me had she ever found out that I had been caught stealing in Lit Brothers. My mother's neighbors, Mr. Murphy, Ms Vernmel Downing, Ms. Gladys Inghram, Ms. Marie Hands, Ms. Greta and her lifelong friends Rose and Buddy had pulled me out of some jams in the past and would do so in the future but I am not sure that they could have if my mother had ever found out and the reason I am able to record this important piece of my life history is because she didn't. They were also two of the people who worked at the Horsman Doll Company.

Trenton at one time was the home for a freight yard of North American Van Lines located on Pashley Avenue. A couple of years after the Lit Brothers problem Bro and I along with three other boys Bruno (Billy), Rudolph and Dorsey would find ourselves in hot water again. This time it was much more serious and would involve the police. The freight yard was our playground, a place we called the "Boxes." The Boxes were actually empty wooden freight containers but they provided one of the best hideouts for a group of young kids from Dunham Street.

The Boxes were our tree houses so to speak. Some of the boxes sat on top of one another and we chose one that nearly hung over the fence facing the railroad tracks where the mounds of rock salt were delivered. It was a two floor duplex and we loved it. We would run through the boxes playing cowboys and Indians or cops and robbers, having the time of our lives. One hot August afternoon we decided to make a campfire just like the cowboys we watched on television. The freight containers were full of the straw type material used to protect whatever product that was being shipped. This straw was what we used to make the campfire as we played. At some point we put the campfire out or so we thought and continued our play. When we emerged from one of the boxes a little while later it was clear that the campfire had not been completely extinguished and one of the boxes was on fire. We hurriedly tried to put it out but it was too late the fire was rapidly spreading from one box to another and we finally decided it was time to get out of there. I remember being the last one to leave but I was really only seconds behind the rest.

We were still there as the fire trucks began to arrive. We even were trying to help them with the fire hoses when we were seen by Mrs. Vernmel (Downing) who lined us up and made us hold hands and marched us onto Dunham Street. She knew we were involved and I think was holding her breath. It was only a short time later that it came to light that we had been seen by people and were identified as the likely culprits. The police came and rounded us up and our parents followed us to the police station at Chancery Lane.

We were eight, ten, ten, eleven and eleven years old, respectively. The youngest of us "Bruno" died in November, 2018. It was the first time any of us had ever been to the police station let alone be questioned by the police. They did the classic thing that police do, they separated us and did the good cop, bad cop thing and tried to pit us against one another by telling us that the boy in the other room had implicated one of us as the one who started the fire. We tried to explain that it happened as an accident and that we would have never intentionally set the Boxes on fire. We loved the Boxes and would have never done anything to destroy our favorite place, our hideout.

As it turned out the entire freight yard of boxes burned to a crisp and a tractor was scorched and damaged and some homes were singed by the fire or smoke. In the end Dorsey ended up in

Juvenile Court and was placed on probation. Why we all weren't is still a mystery and Ms. Vermell, Dorsey's mother was not happy at all with the outcome as Dorsey ended up on probation for a year and Rudolph was forbid from playing with us ever again and he never did for the rest of our growing up, throughout the rest of elementary school, Jr. High School and High School. Bro and I would move on and continue to be friends and buddies for the rest of our lives. What I know today is that children can be coerced by the police to admit doing something they didn't do and I think that's what happened to Dorsey.

Given what this book is about and looking back at the fire in the Boxes and having an adult understanding of the severity of the fire just a few more minutes inside of the boxes and I would not be writing this book but I and the others would have been the earliest of the boys who have passed on as it is clear to me today that we would not have survived the fire. There would have been five little boys from Dunham Street who would have perished in the Boxes fire at the North American Van Lines freight yard.

Dunham Street was a small block of thirty four small three bedroom row houses with basements, first and second floors, a small front yard with modest backyards that were about fifty yards in length. The addresses or numbers on the houses started at 12 and ending at 78.

When I started writing this book it was then and as it had always been, a "dead end" street with one way in and one way out. Today it's no longer a dead end, it has been opened up and new houses have been built on the grounds where the old Gould Battery Factory used to stand. Back then all of the houses were on one side of the street. Across from our homes was the factory where they manufactured batteries, a place that always released a toxic acidic fumes which would choke you.

To this day I am convinced that the cause of many of the deaths of the adults including my mother who died of carcinoma of the lungs and she never was a smoker were the breath taking acidic fumes that bellowed out of the factory . A little more than a decade ago the factory was demolished. There are now new homes that have been recently built that stand where the factory used to be. It has taken years subsequent to the original groundbreaking because of concerns that the ground is toxic and I am of the strong belief that the ground is still toxic.

Dunham Street would claim its share of the boys who would eventually be among the dead. Including Bro. Willis Williams was killed in a car accident in Japan where he was serving in the United States Air Force. Willis was the first and earliest of boys from Dunham Street to die. Levon Kellam Ingram was another of the boys to die. His mother confirmed that he died of a heart attack while living in Brooklyn, New York. There is also Charles Hands who died due to complications associated with diabetes. And there is also Glen Williams and Kenneth Allen, Luther a twin, and William " Bruno" Kidd aka "Billy the Kid," who were boys of Dunham Street. Death has claimed seven boys from Dunham Street, boys who I knew, played with began to grow up with before any of the other boys on the list that I would come to know. It is utterly astounding that a little street like Dunham Street in a small town like Trenton would have lost so many of its sons.

To date there have been nearly two hundred and fifty "Boys of My Summers," known by the writer to have transitioned, whose lives have been cut short by the pathology that has affected and effected all of us, those of us who are gone, and those of us who are still living. By alphabetical order the second boy on the list, Clark Alfred, was one of fifteen boys and ten girls in the first - First Grade Class of the new Monument School opened in September of 1956.

In those days, while the class and the school was predominately black, there were still white children who attended Monument school and three of them, one boy and two girls were in that first grade class. White flight had not completed itself yet in Trenton schools, including elementary, middle, aka, junior high school or high school. In fact, while there were probably no white children in our elementary school after we entered into the fourth grade, all of us attended multi racial middle and high schools. And guess what? It wasn't just different, it was better!

I was a member of that first grade class and so were Billy Carter, Frank Johnson, Henry "Bro" Ellison, aka, "Slim Jenkins"and Gerald "Dinky" Warren, four of the five of my first grade classmates that are members of the list of those who have passed on.

Charles Gerald "Dinky" Warren

(front row right) Clark Alfred, Henry"Bro/Slim Jenkins" Ellison, Jr. (third row left end) Charles Gerald "Dinky" Warren, (top row first left end) Billy Carter, (top row right second from right end) Frank Johnson, Boys from a Monument School 1956 1st grade class.

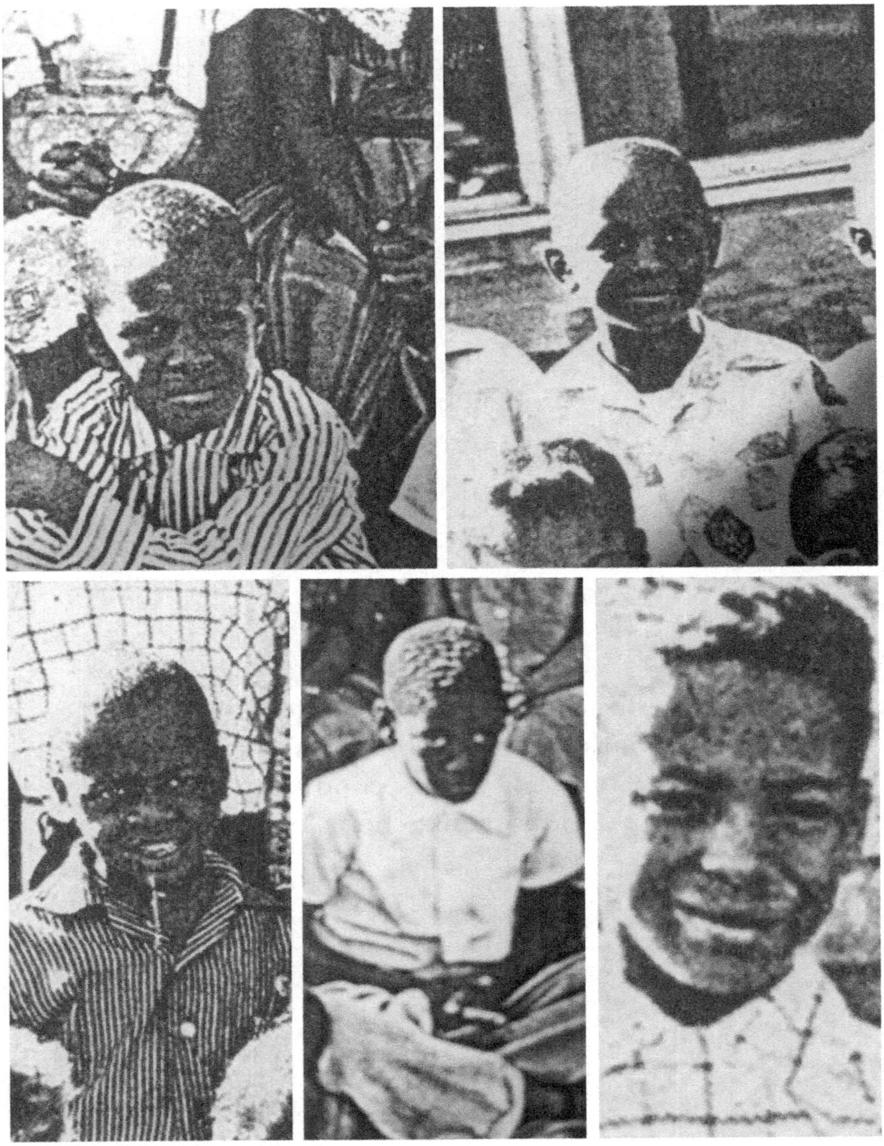

Clark, Frank, Dinky, Bro, Billy

Billy Carter: Member of Monument School's 1st Grade Class of 1956, Trenton, NJ

The "Boys 2 Men" on this list are boys who I went to elementary school, junior high school and high school with, went to Carver Center YMCA with, played basketball, baseball, soccer, ran track, drank with, smoke with, fought with and against, hustled with, traded with, made, loss money with, graduated from high school with, lived and loved with.

Eleven of them; Doug Battle, Freddie Little, Ronald Frost, John Matthews, Harry Smith, Reginald Morrison, Jake Hamilton, Carl Thomas, Jackie Walker, Gregory Jamison, Carlton Carter were members of our high school graduation class of 1969. With exception of Gregory who died in 1993, all of them were deceased by 1989 as their names were announced at the 20th Year High School Reunion of the class of 1969. None of the boys in this group lived to be 40 years old. It is a telling and lasting reminder of how early too many of us have died! As we died our glorious high school was dying with us for much of the same reason, malignant neglect.

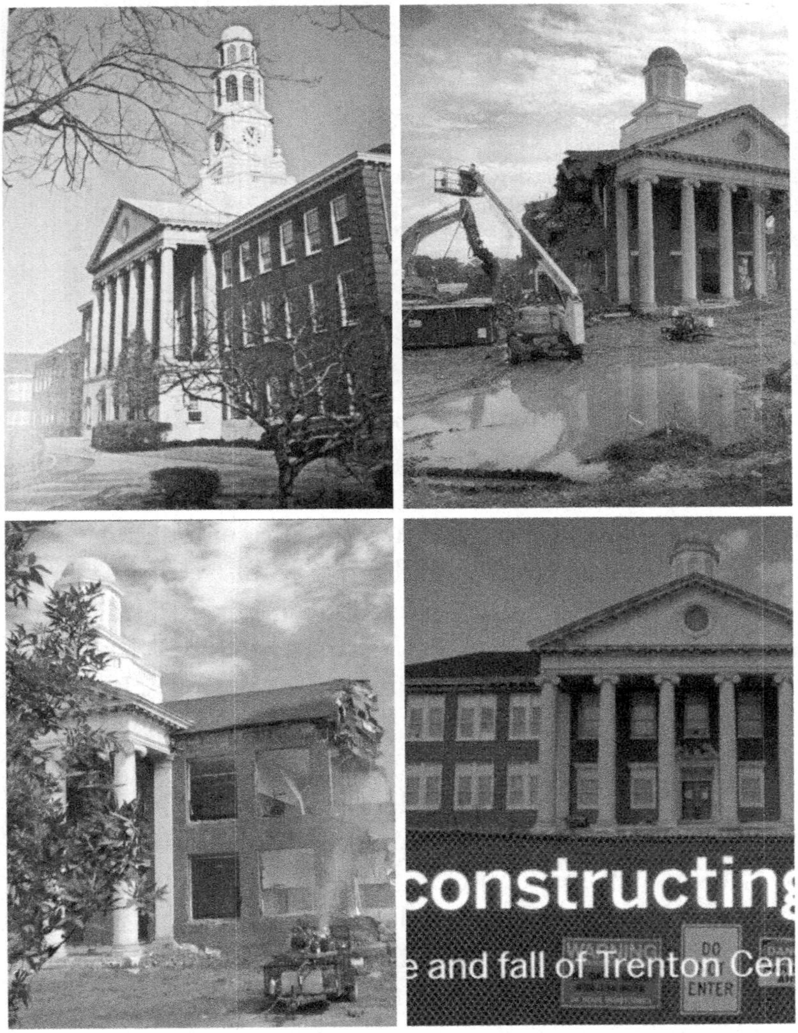

(left to right top) Carlton Carter, John Matthews, Ronald Frost, (center) James "Jake" Hamilton, Frank Johnson, Gregory Jamison, (bottom) Reginald "Zip" Morrison, Guy Westcott, Harry Smith and Carl Thomas

THOMPSON, CARL
620 Hoffman Ave.
Industrial Arts

As aforementioned they are boys who I played basketball with, ran track with, ate lunch in school with. They are boys who I went to the Carver Center YMCA summer day camp with. I went swimming with them at the Ressie and at Hetzel's public swimming pools and at Junior 5 a public junior high school located in North Trenton. We sang in the same choirs together. A plurality of them, were members (Eddie Franklin, Norman Wade, Henry Ellison, Jr., and Steve "Hippie Steve") of Boy Scout Troop 100 at Union Baptist Church on Pennington Avenue.

On our side of town we spent a lot of time at "Muscle Heads" aka Gemes Wade's house on Wilson Street, no matter, if you were a child you were one of his parents children. Once we got to Jr. High School, we gathered at Muss's house every morning to walk the 20 or more blocks to Jr.1.

Jr. High School #1

Glenda, Mike, Mus, Kenny, Apple and Jay coming later, were like sisters and brothers to me and next door was James and Eddie Franklin their cousins Cookie, Red, and Larry, their mothers Ms. Dore and "Ant" Guggua, Bro and me got our first puppies from one of Sally's litter. Sally was not only the Wade family dog but she was everybody's dog unless she got upset with you and she would get upset a lot especially about her puppies.

The Wade Clan (Peterman & Aunt Cochie)

We learned how to dance and Glenda the oldest was our teacher as we prepared to go to parties as we got a little older and started to like and pay more notice to girls. It was a wonderful life. Aunt

Cochie used to scold all of us about washing our "asses!" She'd say that "boys stink to!"

What this book grapples with is the dying of the boys, Mike and Larry were first and James and Eddie; a brother cluster, would die years later yet still not reaching that threescore year and ten threshold, Larry, Mike, James 'Peanut" and Eddie, the boys from Wilson Street have been deceased 20 to 25 years and another boy from Wilson Street, Tommy McCafferty; like too many others, has been gone even longer. There are boys on the list of our dead who died as long as nearly fifty years ago.

Norman Carl "Mike" Wade

We went to the same parties together, the quarter parties with the red lights, dancing to Ooh Baby, Baby and Smokey, I Do Love You, Billie Stewart. I drank wine and beer with many of them. We partied and dance to "Heat Wave" and "Dancing in the Street" and gathered around in awe to watch Rat Antley do the Cha Cha!

One of the other family homes where I spent a lot of time was at Pickett's house; Melvin Douglas Pickett, on Stuyvesant Avenue. Picket, Tank (Stanley), Tony (Anthony) Lomon and Karl Teape and of course the matriarch of the house Ms. Mildred the mother of "Doug," Tank and Tony. She was a mother who didn't mind giving any and all of us a tongue lashing to put it lightly! And I can hear her calling downstairs to tell us it was getting late and we needed to get out of her house, 'go home!" And while we eventually obeyed her command it was hard because we were playing tonk and blackjack jack for pennies while eating pizzas and having a ball in a time of our innocence. None of us could have imagined on those nights of any of us dying. While all of us will leave here, we all will die, it is still hard to grasp that so many of us would die so young and be dead for so long and almost none of us to date living to be 70 years old.

We smoked cigarettes (Larks, Montclair's, Salem's, Parliaments, Winston's, we tried Camels, Pall Mall and Chesterfield's and Kools) together for the first time and later on we smoked "reefer" together and a long list of us would go on to use other drugs together including Trenton's first; childhood drug epidemic, sniffing glue. In fact I don't know of any boys I grew up with who sniffed glue who did not also go on to use heroin. So for many of us cigarettes and glue were the so-called, "stepping stone" drugs.

Eighteen of them (Karl, Eddie, Wayne, Big Doug, Freddie, Bo, Furman, Little Alfred, Cliffy, Bubby, Slim Jenkins, Tank, Lee Grant, Sultan, Dinky, Jimmy, Bob and Arthur McCrea were members; there were 40 members, of Second To None (STN), the best youth social club in the history of Trenton, New Jersey. These boys represent more than forty percent (45%) of the members of our beloved club. It is absolutely astonishing to me that all of these guys are no longer with us. And what is even more troubling is that the last five of the six of them to die, Tank born in 1953 died in 2009 at age 56, Lee Grant, Sultan and Dinky died in their early 60's, Jimmy and Kenneth " Country," were the oldest of any of the boys in our club to die transitioning at ages 66 and 67, respectively. In fact they died older than the overwhelming majority of the two hundred and fifty plus Boys named herein who have died.

Who were all of these boys and what were they? The following is the list of who they were and what were they is a story that is as profound as the dying syndrome that these black sons of Trenton, New Jersey have experienced and those of us left behind who remember them. Their deaths speak to truth as they *"Bear Witness in Mortality, Because the Truth Is Spoken Here."*

Throughout this treatise there are photos taken on May 2, 2015, where the surviving Boys of Our Summers met and gathered at the hallowed stomping ground at the "5 Points." We came because we responded to a call, we came to see one another and to talk to each other, to hug, to laugh, to cry and to reminisce and to be with one another again, even if only for a little while. We came to call out the names of those who have left us, many of them a long time ago, so long ago that some were awed and wowed that they had forgotten about some of those on the list. Some of us; I foremost among them, hadn't seen one another in decades. some who came that day had spent years, some two decades behind the walls and inside of the prison industrial complex.

There were those who came out like "*Nose*" and "*Pop*" who have been inseparable all of their lives. There were others like Haywood Mckenzie, father of former New York Giant, Super Bowl Champion, Kareem Mckenzie. Many may have forgotten that but for a near life ending automobile accident Haywood would have been one of the most sought after college basketball recruits in the nation and there is no doubt in this writer's mind that he would have played in the National Basketball Association. One of the "Boys;" Charles "Dino" Holman, whose presence we lost for nearly 20 years was there that day. Brucie Carmichael, Belvin Melvin, Johnny Baker, George "GG" Gaines (Muhammad), Larry

"PoBob" Housley, Tyrone George (now deceased as of 2018), Andrew "Gump" Rawson, Stanley Yates, Eugene "Breezy" Briggs, Alton "Red Chief"Grier, Freddie Grier, Lee Davis, Ervin Higginbotham, the Nixon brothers, Melvin Hopps and a long list of others. Six of the Boys who were there that day; Alton, Eli, Leslie, Lee, Amos "BoBo and Tyrone, have since transitioned as have a number of the Boys since that date, Scotty, Hamp, Snap and Felton Smith, Bruce, Gregg, Carl, Willie, and William "Bruno" among them.

"Nose" (right) Brucie Carmichael (left)

"Pop"

Haywood McKenzie

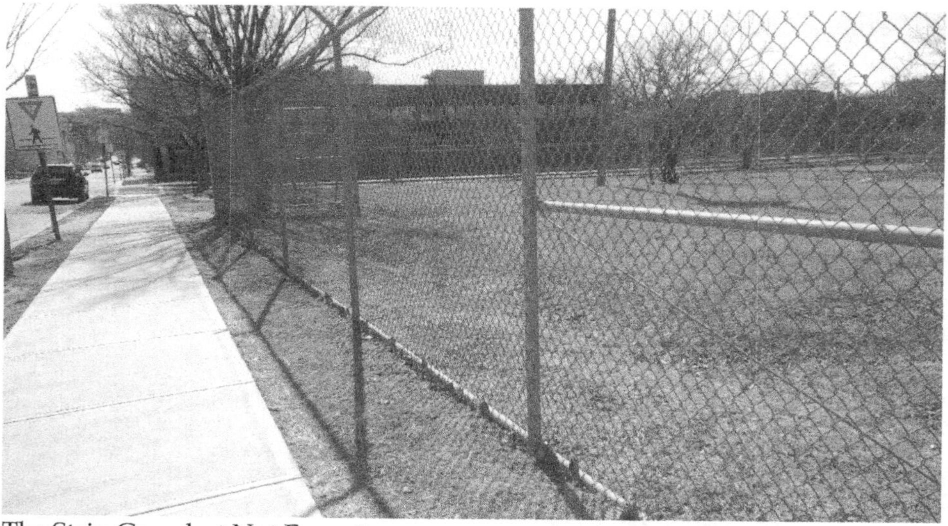

The Strip Gone but Not Forgotten

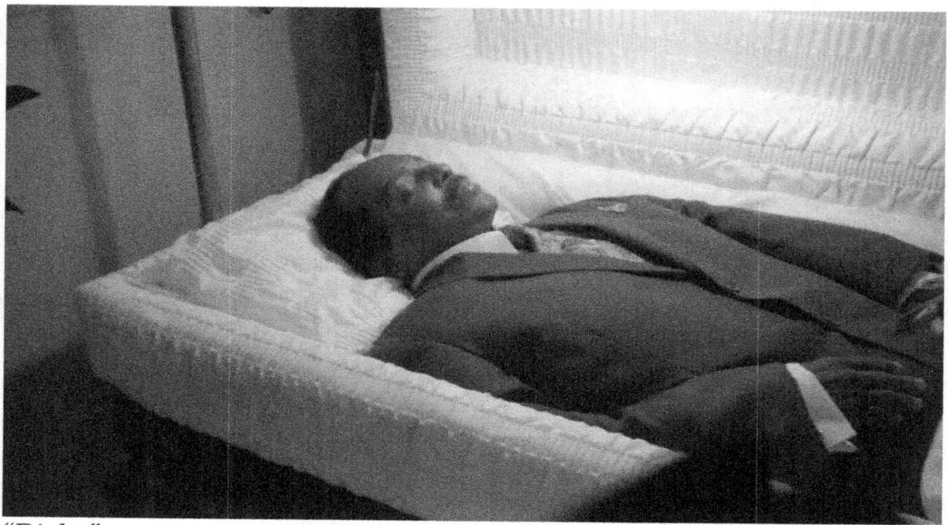

"Dinky"

A Celebration of Life
For Our Beloved

Sunrise
April
21, 1951

To Glory
October
31, 2015

We were never ready to say goodbye
To someone we hold so near
If we had any say in it, you would still be here
But God had his reason He had a plan
And we know you're in His mighty hands.

Ralph R. Downing Jr.

~ Service ~

Saturday, October 7, 2015 at 12:00 p.m.

Hughes Funeral Home
324 Bellevue Avenue
Trenton, New Jersey 08618
Pastor Edward Blue,
Officiating

"Stick"

1 Clifford Adams
2. Clark Alfred
3. Roscoe Alfred]

4. William "Billy" Allen]
5. Frankie Allen]

6. Wayne Allen (HIV)
7. Kenneth "Red" Allen

8. Joe Anderson (TNJ)

9. Clifford "Cliffy" Armstrong (Homicide)]
10. Ronald Armstrong]
11. Stanley Armstrong]
12. Nate "The Great" Armstrong
13. Robert "Rat" Antley (Homicide)

14. Doug "Big Doug" Battle (Kidney Disease)]
15. Terry "Mope" Battle]

16. Muhammed "Red" Berry

17. Willie Berry
18. Charles "Banny" Berry

19. John "Bo" Bethea

20. William "Big Bill"Thompson (Complications of Diabetes)

21 Kenneth "Mule Train" Bethea (Drug/Poisoning)]
22. Eli "Little Eli" Bethea]

23. Carl Black
24. Levi "Tony" Blackwell
25.Vernon Bond (Accidental Suicide)
26.. Larry Bostik (Homicide)
27. Bradley Boyd (Heart Disease)
28. Alphonso Briggs
29. James "JB" Brown
30. Michael "Little Michael" Brown

31. Craig Bruce]
32. Jeffrey Bruce]
33. Leslie Bruce]

35. Matthew Brunson
36. Lester Buchanan
37. Bobby Bynum
38. Bubby Byrd (Cavalier)
39. Carlton Carter

40. Donald "The Fox" Carter
41. Ralph "Pumpkin" Carter

42. Tyrone Carter
43 Butch Clark] (Homicide)
44. Donald Clark] (Drug Suicide)

45. Frank Clark (HIV)

46. Tony Clark
47. Charles "Big Junie" E. Coles, Jr.
48. Butch Cooper
49 Furman Counts (Homicide)

50. George Dash
51. Willie Dash

52. Bruce Davis]
53. Kenny Davis]

54. Wille "Blue Chip" Davis (Homicide) (#229 Lee Davis)

55. Butch Denson]
56. Jesse Denson]

57. Marvin Dotson
58. Ralph Ricky "Stick" Downing. Jr.
59. Cornell Dukes
60. Henry "Bro-Slim Jenkins" Ellison, Jr.
61. Robert Echoes (Homicide)

62. Dale Fitzgerald]
63. David Fitzgerald]

64. Charles Edward "Eddie" Franklin
65. James Franklin

66. Larry "Little Larry" Franklin
67. Ronald Frost
68. Jeffrey Gaines

69. John “Denny” Glover]
70. Obedia “Bunky” Glover]
72. James “Jimmy” Glover] (STN)

73. Jeffrey Goss (Drug/Suicide)

74. Robert “Bobby” Grier]
75. Alton “Red Chief” Grier](Cavalier)

75. James (Jake) Hamilton (Class of 1969)
76. Charles Hands (Diabetes)

77. Larry Hightower]
78. Michael Hightower]
79.O.C. Hightower]

80. Willie “Jumpy” Hightower
81. David Hill (Diabetes)
82. Jimmy Hill
83. Roy Hodges
84. Leonard Hood

85. Earnest Housley]
86. William “Clutch” Housley]
87. Michael Housley (Liver Disease)]

88. Boyd “Skippy” Howard
89. Henry “Head” Hudson (Complications of Addiction)
90. Gregory “Chilly Hassan” Hunt (Died at Trenton State Prison)
91.Wallace Huntley (Complications of Addiction)
92. Levon Kellam Ingram(Heart Attack)

93. Ervin Jackson (HIV)
94. Peanut Jackson

95.. Gregory Jamison (Drug/Poisoning)
96. Frank Johnson (Homicide)
97. Willie Johnson
98. Steve (Hippie Steve) Jones
99. Tyrone Kelly
100. Bruce "Kitch" Kitchen
101. John Paul Lacey (Homicide)
102. Fredrik Little (Brain Aneurysm) (Class of 1969)
103. George "Kobo" Locket (Drug/Suicide)
104. Stanley "Tank" Loman
105. Francis Xavier Lee
106. Warren "Squirrel" Levrett
107. Gary Livingston
108. Billy McARoy
109. Peter "Petey" Mason
110. John Matthews
111. Tommy McCafferty (Suicide)
112. James "Bubby" McKenzie
113. Edward (Fat June Bug) McKinney

114. Donald "Duck" McNeil]
115. Fletcher "Big Fletch" McNeil]
116. Reginald "Reggie" McNeil]
117. Gerald "Big Mug/Smash"McNeil

118. Steven "Scotty" Miller (INSTANT FUNK) (Cavalier)
119. Joshua (Joshmo) Moore (Homicide)
120. Ronald "Zip' Morrison (Suicide)(Class of 1969)

121. Lee Grant Moses
122. Rayfield "Jug" Meyers
123. Richard Nixon (Homicide)
124. Darrell Nolan
125. Earl Nolan]
126. Floyd Nolan (Homicide)
127. Charles "Slim" Oliver (Stroke)

128. Jimmy Patterson]
129. Scoffield Patterson]
130. Earl Pernell (Heart Disease)
131. Juan "Kopek" Perry
132. Horace Phelps
133.Doug Posey (Diabetes)
134.James Ransom (Homicide)
135. Donnie "Sultan" Ray

136.Fred Robinson]
137. Jackie Robinson]

138. Don Roberson
139. Ronnie Robinson
140. Jerry Rucker
141. James "Porky" Russell
142. Tommy Rose (Motor Vehicle Accident)
143. Willie "Billy" Sanders, Jr.
144. Carl Sally
145. Jody Williams (Cavalier)
146. Toby Scrivens
147. Calvin Small (Suicide)
148. Dexter Smith
149. Elsie "El Sid" Smith (Drug/Poisoning)(Cavalier)

150. Melvin "Mel" Smith} (Drug/Poisoning)
151. Ricky Smith}

152.[Harry Smith]
153. [Lenny Smith]
154. Wayne Smith

155. Quinton Smith, Jr.
156. Lee Grant Snead
157. Kenny Snow
158. Stanley "Doc" Stroman (Heart Disease)
159. John "Stulu" Steward
160. David "Butch" Taylor
161. Earl Taylor (HIV)

162. Jimmy "Jimmy Rob" Robinson
163. Ronnie "Juice" Robinson

164. Karl Teape (Drug/Poisoning)
165. Carl Thomas (Class of 1969)

166. Ezekiel "Zeke" Thomas (Drug/Suicide)]
167. Earl "Moon" Thomas (Drug/Suicide)]
168. Ronald "Ham" Thomas]
169. Charles "Charlie Bird" Thomas]

170. James "Crazy Jack" Thomas
171. William "Big Bill/Mr. Bill" Thompson
172. Milton Tucker (Drug/Suicide)
172. Bobby Turner (Homicide)
173. Norman "Mike" Wade

174. Sam Ward
175. Jackie Walker (Accidental Drowning) (Class of 1969)
176. Gerald "Dinky" Warren
177. Rufus "Butch" Watkins (Drug/Suicide)
178. Guy Westcott (Class of 1969)

179. Jody White]
180. Sam White]

181. Alvin "Junie" Wilkins

182. Alfred "Little Alfred" Williams]
182. Anthony Williams (Homicide)]

183. Melvin "Little Melvin" Williams
184. Willis Williams (Motor vehicle accident)
185. Bobby William (#234 Gregg 'Hammer" Williams)
186. Glen Williams

187. Eugene "Wimp" Woodson
188. Eli Woodson

189. David "Butch" Taylor

190. "Snap" Smith
191. Felton "Bruiser"Smith

192. Reggie Graves
193. Harvey Lowe
194. William "Billy" Carter
195. Alvin "Block" Tillery

196. Anthony “Tony” Lomon (Brother of Stanley “Tank” Lomon)

197. Lance Hodges
198. Lance White
199. Dwight Bramley

200. Charlie Bethea (Cavalier)
201. Wayne Bethea (Cavalier)
202. Robert “Junie Babe” Bethea

203. Lester “Peppy” Presley
204. Obie English
205. Waymond Jackson
206. Timmy McCall
207. Al Stroman (TNJ)

208. Anthony Figueroa
209. Carlos Figueroa

210. Leroy King (Cavalier)
211. James “Deany” Jones (Cavalier)
212. Jesse Logan (Cavalier)
213. Charles “JB” Haywood(Cavalier)
214. Charles Coley (Cavalier)
215. Charles Belcher (Cavalier)
216. Felix “Monk” Slaughter (Cavalier)
217. Ronnie Denson (Cavalier)
218. Joe Thorpe (Cavalier)
219. James “Jimmy” Laramore (Suicide) (Cavalier)
220. Ernest “Little Geech” Scott
221. Lewis Garvin

222. Timmy McCall
223. James McCall

224. Hampton "Hamp"Jenks
225. Tommy Aikens
226. Henry Wayman
227. Jimmy Nunley
228. Charles Tuner
229. Lee Davis (Class of 1969)
230. Bruce Nixon

231. Ernie Johnson
232. Jamie Johnson
233. Eugene Johnson

234. Gregg "Hammer" Williams/(#185-Bobby Williams)

235. Harry "Goody" Goodman

236. Bob McCrea
237. Arthur McCrea

238. Warren "Speedy" Spady
239. Willie Walker
240. Charles "Chuckie" Nelson

241. Terry Brown/(#30-Michael Brown)

242. Chubby Blackwell/(#24-Levi "Tony"Blackwell)

243. Tyrone George
244.. Willie Davis (Class of 1969)
245. Henry Douglas (Class of 1969)
246. Amos "BoBo" Dean
247. William "Bruno"Kidd
248. Carl McCall (Cavalier)
249. Joseph B, Harlan (Trenton Riot of 1968; Killed by the Police)
250. Charles "Tex" Boston
251. James "Peanut" Johnson(Wilson Street Boy)
252. Kenneth "Country" Griffin (Cancer) [STN]

The names and numbers above also represent forty-four (44) clusters of brothers representing ninety-five boys on the list; the Alfred bothers, two sets of Allen brothers; Billy and Frankie; Wayne and Kenneth, Armstrong's, Battle's, Blackwell's, two sets of Bethea brothers; Kenneth and Eli; Charlie, Wayne and Robert, Brown's Terry and Michael, Bruce's, Carter's, Clark's, Dash's, Denson's, two sets of Davis', Figueroa's, Fitzgerald's, Franklin's, Glover's, Grier's, Housley's, Jackson's, Johnson's, Lomon's, McCall's, McCrea's, McNeil's, Nolan's, Patterson's, two sets of Robinson brothers, three sets of Smith brothers, Thomas', White's, Williams', and Woodson's.

The fact that forty-four clusters of brothers, in some cases; like the McNeil's, the Housley's and the Thomas,' all hailing from Prospect Village, have lost nearly an entire family of brothers, save one, respectively. Larry "PoBob" Housley, Leroy " Winnie" Thomas and "Doc" McNeil are the only boys left of their siblings. PoBob having lost Ernest, Earl and Michael; Winnie having lost Earl, Ronald, Charles and Ezekiel, and Doc having lost Reginald, Donald, Fletcher and Gerald. Each of them represents the ***"Last Man Standing"*** springing from a brood of siblings who have flown away, having succumbed to morbidity factors such as diabetes, complications associated with the chronic consumption of alcohol and addiction to the drug alcohol, the ravages of and the consequences of heroin addiction including heroin poisoning (aka: overdose), and kidney disease.

Larry "PoBob" Housley (*A Last Brother Standing*)

Gregg "Hammer" Williams

William "Bruno" Kidd

Billy Allen (younger brother of Frankie Allen/Carver Center Boys

Billy and Mary Allen

As of this writing, there are two hundred forty-three "Boys of My Summers" who have passed through this life. These numbers are extraordinary for a small town like Trenton and I am certain that there are more. I have talked to and interviewed men who were born and raised in large cities like New York, Philadelphia and Chicago and I have yet to talk to anyone of them of my generation or younger, who could say that they can count two hundred forty-three boys that they knew who were dead. And in the case of Philadelphia and Chicago having, historically, long histories of gang problems and no one I've talked to from these two cities can match the numbers recorded in the small town where I grew up.

Juan "Kopeck" Perry

These deaths not only represent an extraordinary impact on a city but it also represents an extraordinary impact on families, especially. The fact that more than two hundred and fifty black men; all of them members of my generation and most of them who would have been my age, have lost their lives in Trenton, leaves us with literally hundreds of children and in a plurality of instances, grand children who have had to grow up without their fathers and grandfathers and in more than enough instances they are children who grew up without knowing very much at all about their fathers. Such is the case of N'Gai Scrivens, a young cousin of mine whose father "Billy" Sanders died when he was just months old. Billy who was my older cousin and N'Gai's father died in 1972 at age 24, nearly half a century ago. He died inside of the newly built station of the Trenton Police Department on North Clinton Avenue. The cause of death was by hanging. While there were many who believed that he may have been killed by the Police, I and other family members believed that it was a completed suicide. Sometime after Billy's death N'Gai's mother (Kim) would come to love another Trenton boy and lifelong friend Jimmy Laramore.

Billy Sanders

Jimmy Laramore

Jimmy grew up just around the corner from me on Pennington Avenue. While there were people who moved to other streets, blocks, wards and neighborhoods most families that I came to know lived in the same house, on the same street, in the same Ward for decades and some of the children of our parents still do. Sometime about 2016 I'd receive a phone call from his son N'Gai that Jimmy had died. Initially N'Gai didn't tell me that his step-father had committed suicide. A short time later I would learn from another life long friend Andrew aka Andy "Gump" Rawson that Jimmy had actually died by suicide. I later called N'Gai to confirm what I had been told and he answered in the affirmative that suicide was indeed Jimmy's cause of death.

Jimmy

In hindsight, while discussing this book with Jimmy he inquired about making a contribution to the mental health disorders that is affecting so many of us, sadly we never got to it, yet through his living and his death he has made a profound contribution bearing witness to the hidden and near silent epidemic of the mental health crisis in the African American diaspora in this country.

Throughout our childhoods I lived on Dunham Street, just three short streets around two corners. We'd known each other forever and he was one of the nicest cats that I have ever met. Jimmy would become good friends with my step brother, Frances Xavier Lee also on the list and the rest of their crew, James Franklin; also on the list, A.J. Tibbs, Horace Hamilton and Willie "Blue Chip" Davis. With exception of A.J. and Horace the rest have have also died "Blue Chip" being the first of them and the earliest murder victim among the boys who were murdered. while his death was a result of his involvement in an attempted robbery, he and his crime partner, "Spook Juice," his murder was declared to be justified.

Jimmy and N'Gai's mother would marry and they would also leave Trenton to plant roots in Toledo, Ohio.

That sadly and tragically; beyond imagination, Jimmy would also die as a victim of his own hands, cause of death, suicide by hanging is mind boggling and beyond comprehension, especially because two men; both of them, who were attached to N'Gai in life, death and life and in death again, although their deaths coming some forty-five years apart, it is an eerie and unbelievable set of tragic circumstances.

Police Station Clinton Avenue (1972)

Billy Sanders & Barbara

The children of Milton Tucker and Jackie Walker grew up without their fathers and I had an opportunity to meet both of them at a celebration of life gathering in Trenton some years ago.

We have been living in a time when many people point to the absence of black men with regard to their communities in general, their families in particular and in the lives of their children especially. Oftentimes we point to the number of black men who are in prisons and jails in America. But we leave out the fact that many of the men in prison are in touch with their children, see their children on a fairly regular basis and are involved in their children's lives inclusive of being the best parent that they possibly can while in prison.

The New York Times: 1.5 Million "Black Men Missing"

The New York Times says this, *"In New York (where I have lived and worked), almost 120,000 black men between the ages of 25 and 54 are missing from everyday life. In Chicago, (a city where I have studied) 45,000 are, and more than 30,000 are missing in Philadelphia " (a city where I have also lived and worked).*
"They are missing, largely because of early deaths or because they are behind bars."

The larger and real problem is that the absence of black men in the community and in the lives of their children have more to do with excess and premature death than it has to do with their being incapacitated by incarceration in prison and jails. especially where Trenton is concerned. A plurality of the "missing" from Trenton have been missing for more than 40 years or nearly a half century.

The latter is plus the fact that most of those who are in prisons and jails will be coming home at some point. And even when they do make it home form long periods of incarceration, they come home to die like "Butch" Taylor who died less than two years after leaving prison and after being "down" nearly twenty years. But death is an absolute and permanent thing that has tens of thousands of black children who grow up without their fathers. There are any number of the boys from Trenton who were taken away from us for decades yet their incarceration was not permanent and they returned home to be with their children and grandchildren.

The NYT article also says this: "*Perhaps the starkest description of the situation is this: More than one out of every six black men who today should be between 25 and 54 years old have disappeared from daily life.*"

Perhaps it is because by age 25 homicide had been a leading cause of death for a decade prior to having turned 25 for the 15-25 year old age group added to the fact that homicide continues to be a leading cause of death for black men up to and until age 54. Add to the latter; according to the Center for Disease Control and Prevention, that death due to HIV/AIDS had become a leading cause of death for those of us 25 to 44 in the 1990's, more than two decades ago.

The boys named herein are represented by forty-four clusters of brothers. The Armstrong brothers, Cliffy, Stanley and Ronald, of Brunswick Avenue make up one of the clusters. The clusters also include the Alford brothers, Clark and Roscoe, the Nolan brothers, Darrell, Earl and Floyd of North Trenton, the Allen brothers, Wayne and Kenneth "Red," David and Jimmy Hill and more.

Prospect Village; a public housing complex, located in Northwest Trenton was particularly devastated as it relates to brother clusters who have passed. They include the Thomas brothers, Earl, Ronald, Charles and Ezekiel, the Housley brothers Michael, William "Clutch" and Ernest "Puddin," the McNeil brothers Reggie, Donald "Duck," Fletcher and Gerald "Big Mug/Smash" and the Williams brothers Alfred and Anthony, all of Prospect Village.

There are also brothers Jody and Sam White and Butch and Donald Clark of South Trenton, Doug and Terry Battle of Burton Avenue in North Trenton and Harry, Lenny and Wayne Smith of East Trenton, the Bruce brothers, Craig, Jeffrey and Leslie, the Lomon brothers, Stanley "Tank" and Tony, The McCrea brothers Bob and Arthur, the Smith brothers Mel and Ricky from Pennington Avenue in North Trenton, the Robinson brothers Ronnie "Juice" and Jimmy "Rob," another set of Smith brothers "Snap" and Felton, the Patterson brothers Jimmy and Scoffield, the Robinson brothers from Wilbur Section, Fred and Jackie, the Grier's Bobby and Alton, Eddie and James Franklin, John "Denny." Obedia "Bunky" and James "Jimmy" Glover, Frankie and Billie Allen, are two brothers that I met when I was six or seven years old at the Carver Center Summer Day Camp. We would meet there every summer for years on end. In fact the Carver Center YMCA was a hub for hundreds of boys from our era and generation, scores of them among the list of those passed, had a connection to and relationship with Carver Center. And there are few among us who do not know the name of and heard the voice of the late Honorable Lanny Butler, Sr. who did his best to whisper something favorable in our ears, "dropping jewels"and "pulling the coat" of boys, one boy at a time, boys from every ward and every part of Trenton.

An Institution: Carver Center YMCA 40 Fowler Street, Trenton, New Jersey 08618

Mr. Lanny Butler, Sr. (Heart & Soul of Carver Center YMCA)

Sheila Sherman-Baldwin & FRIENDS OF CLIFFORD
presents a
BANQUET FOR
THE LATE GREAT
Clifford Adams
A CELEBRATION OF LOVE
MARCH 8, 2015 • 4pm-9pm
TICKETS: $50.00
DRESS TO IMPRESS
DINNER, TRIBUTE, and ENTERTAINMENT
Contact Sheila Sherman-Baldwin for ticket info (609) 954-6440
CLIFFORD ADAMS WAS ONE OF OUR OWN
NOTTINGHAM FIREHOUSE BALLROOM
200 MERCER STREET.
MERCERVILLE, NEW JERSEY 08690
*ALL PROCEEDS WILL BENEFIT THE MEDICAL AND OTHER EXPENSES INCURRED

Clifford Adams (Kool & The Gang)

These were not ordinary boys but one of the most extraordinary, talented, smart, and funny group of scholars, comedians, barbers, entertainers, sports athletes and more, that the world didn't get a chance to see, hear, or experience.

(Center) Muhammed "Red" Berry one of the best young fighters on the planet (top left) a survivor Bernard Porter, Sr.

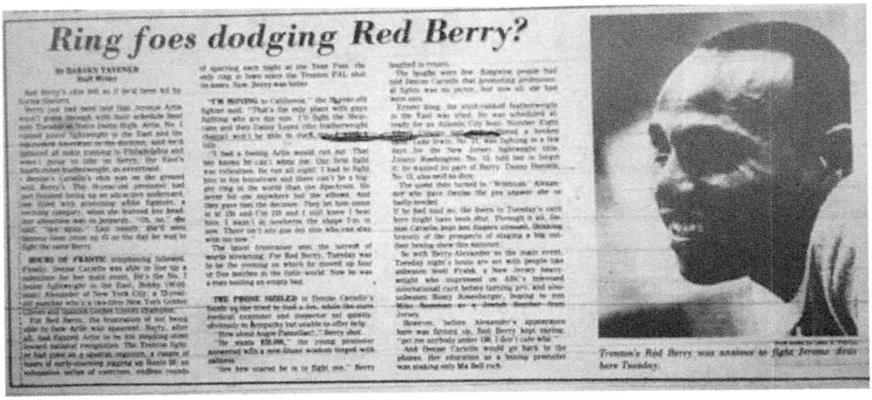

Ring foes dodging Red Berry?

Trenton's Red Berry was anxious to fight Jerome Artis here Tuesday.

Muhammad "Red" Berry

This is not a book about bad boys but a book about boys who had some bad things happen to them, boys who had dreams, who were loved and who loved in return.

In Loving Memory
of Our Beloved

Kenneth Allen Jr.

Sunrise
cember 13, 1951

Sunset
June 03, 2015

Service:
Monday, June 19, 2015 at 11:00 A.M.

Hughes Funeral Home
324 Bellevue Avenue
Trenton, New Jersey 08618

Reverend Keith A. Marshall, Pastor
Macedonia Baptist Church,
Officiating

Anthony "Tony" Lomon: Author, Teacher

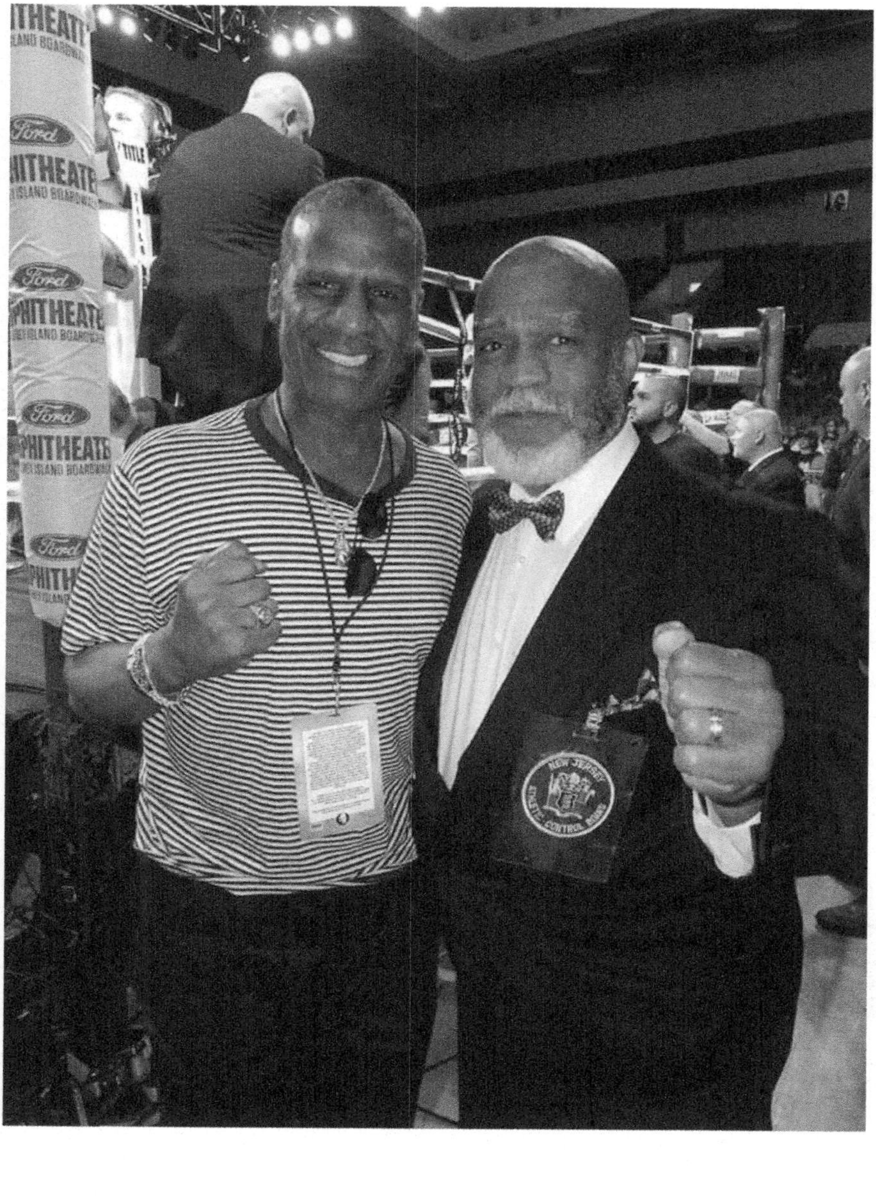
Ford

mes
EJ
Al
Joe

(left to Right) Saoul Mamby (WBC Junior Welterweight Champion 1980-82) with one of the survivors, Trenton's own, Lindsey "Butch/Monster" Page

Obie English (A Trenton Heavyweight)

Clark Alford was one of the best, boy gymnast in Trenton, New Jersey, and he might have been one of the best pre-teen gymnast in the country. As a tumbler I don't think that there were many kids in the gymnastic world who could have competed with him. And anyone who knew him and who had seen him in action would not dispute my words. The Olympics weren't on the horizon for young kids in Trenton, at least not in gymnastics but had they been Clark Alfred would have been an Olympic athlete, no doubt.

Clark Alford

Then we had the scholars among the group. Most notably was Ezekiel "Zeke" Thomas was foremost among them. Zeke was awarded a full academic scholarship at La Salle University in Philadelphia, Pa. La Salle was then and is now one of the most prestigious Universities in the City of Philadelphia, the state of Pennsylvania and the nation. In fact all of the Thomas brothers were academically inclined, which is an understatement. These dudes were straight smart, actually brilliant. I was in class once with "Charlie Bird" the youngest of the five Thomas brothers. We were in the eighth grade and he had his head down on the desk and was actually sleeping. Our math teacher Mr. Hogan woke him up to a math problem he had on the board. This was an attempt by the teacher to embarrass him for sleeping but it was a big mistake on the teacher's part. Bird woke up looked at the problem, dissected it in a matter of what seemed like seconds, answered the problem correctly and went back to sleep.

The teacher was so stunned he didn't even bother to scold him about putting his head back down on the desk let alone that he'd gone back to sleep. Having your head down on your desk during class when we were going to school was a violation of profound significance and warranted disciplinary action or at the very least that the student be embarrassed.

The Thomas brothers were not your typical nerds. These were boys who were raised in Prospect Village, a rough public housing project and they didn't necessarily act like the typical smart kid and they never flaunted it. These were boys, teenagers and men who were "slick," who shot crap on the sidewalk with the rest of us or should I say shot what was known as "Teas" which were bad dice or crooked dice (ace four fives, deuce trey sixes, ace trey fives, four trey miss outs and six ace flats) dice that always made the numbers you wanted them too. Moon the oldest brother was a fly, sharp, slick, skilled hustler but a gifted scholar as well. But the Thomas brothers weren't the only scholars in this group. James "Bubby" McKenzie was another of the smartest academics known us. Bubby was smart, he could figure out stuff or breakdown what the teacher was talking about with amazing precision and he was an intellectual. He was one of these guys who always carried around a newspaper, like the New York Times or something.

We'd ask Bubby - what the fuck are you doing with the New York Times?– just joking, we knew what he was doing, analyzing the times, the news which we'd break down over an intellectual moment that we tended to have throughout any given day.

Bubby

Furman Counts was also another of our academic scholars, intellectuals and sophisticated cats who we knew and loved. Furman, who we called "Charles Lloyd", after the jazz artist, was a young teenage jazz connoisseur. Furman is the boy who introduced all of us to Yusef Lateef and a tune called "Number 7." Furman was into John Coltrane and Miles Davis and demonstrated a sophistication of jazz that was way beyond his years. As I think about it; what things were worth then and what they might be worth now, Furman had a collection of jazz albums that would have been worth a fortune today. At the time this all was happening to us we were all fifteen, sixteen and seventeen year olds. Lee Grant Moses was another scholar. While he was handsome, sharp, witty, clever he was also smart in school despite the fact he could; and would, also fight he was brilliant in the classroom.

Rufus "Butch" Watkins was one of my boyhood heroes. He was not any older than I was but he stood out in a way that forever impressed me. He was about five nine or ten in height and was one of the most handsome boys that I'd known. He had an Evander Holyfield type physic. Like many of the boys/men on the list Rufus was cool. But the difference was that he was cool without even trying to be so. Rufus was a great athlete and the girls loved him. He played basketball, soccer, and ran track for Junior High School #1. He also boxed for P.A.L AAU Boxing team coached by Percy Richardson and was a Golden Gloves Champ at 160lbs. As cool as he was, he never flaunted it. He was actually a soft spoken, quiet and reserved kind of guy. But he was also a boy to be reckoned with, simply put, Rufus could fight and most everybody knew he could and those who were less knowledgeable about him in this area would pay for it if they mistakenly crossed his path. One of my favorite memories and stories about Rufus was when we both played on the soccer team for Jr. 1. I was an eighth grader at the time and he Rufus was in the ninth grade.

It was my first year on the team as I didn't go out for the team as a seventh grader for lack of confidence. I wasn't yet a starter but I would become one that year. Mr. Preston, our coach was preparing our team for a big game. The game was going to be played against our arch rival, Junior High School #2. Junior 2 was the reigning city soccer champions and had beat our team in our first meeting of the year at our field. The game was pretty rough and tensions were high and there were a few times during the game that players had to be separated.

Giving credit where it is due, Jr. 2 had a great team with great players which included the Stellitano brothers all of who were top notch soccer stars at our level and all of them including the oldest brother John would go on to be stars at the high school level. Frank
Stellitano, who I played against would become member of the Trenton Italian mob and years later; 1979, would be found in the trunk of a car at the Philadelphia airport killed by Sammy "The Bull" Gravano the Underboss of the Gambino crime family.The rumor was that when our team visited Jr. 2 that there was going to be trouble, either before, during or after the game. As practice ended the day before the game Mr. Preston gathered us together for a lecture and a warning. Because he knew of the rumor, his warning to the team was that "if there is a fight and anybody on our team throws a punch they can turn in their uniform." Quietly, in a soft tone, but loud enough for any of the players to hear him Rufus said,"if anybody hits me, I'm gonna be fighting and taking off my uniform at the same time." And anyone in ear shot knew that he meant it. As much as I respected Mr. Preston, on this day I was not only impressed with Rufus but I felt protected and because I wanted to be like him, had anyone hit me that day, I would been doing what Rufus did. It turned out that we did come into hostile territory but we left unscathed except that we lost a hard fought game to Jr. 2 because they were just that good and again that year they would go on to be city champions and we would take second spoils which meant little to nothing. There was no trophy for second place.

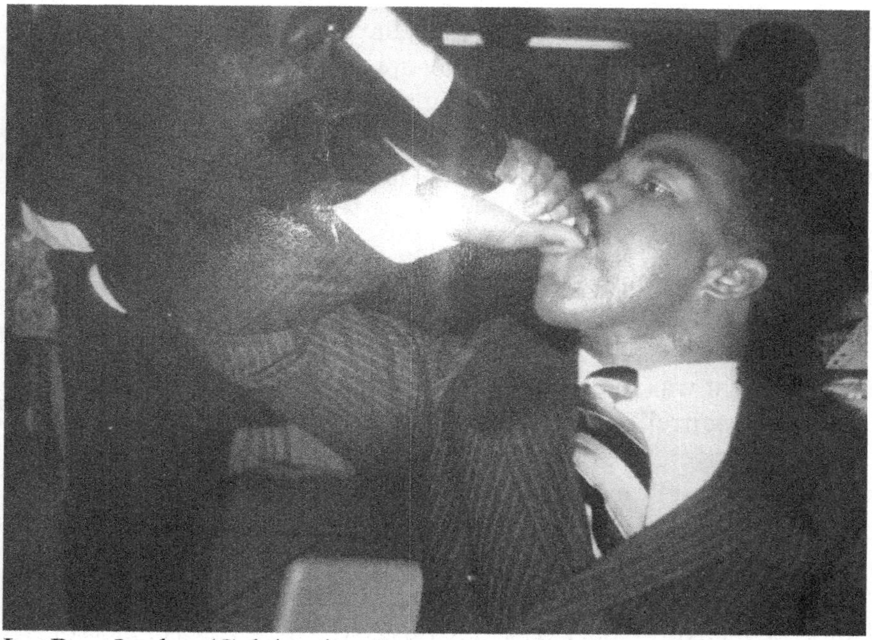

LeeRoy Jordan (Celebrating Recovery w/Sparkling Apple Cider 1987)

My other hero on the list was a boy by the name of Frank Clark. Frank Clark by all measures would be considered a little guy. But he was actually a little big guy. Frank was one of those people in our world who exude all the features of the adage that "it ain't the size of the dog in the fight but the size of the fight in the dog." Frank was a sports superstar at both the Junior High School and High School levels. While it didn't seem like it then, Frank was about 5'5" in height. I guess because I had so much admiration for him he seemed taller. But it was also because whatever he played, basketball, baseball or soccer, he played it taller than he actually was. Frank was a light skinned kid, with so called "good hair." The good hair thing was about our not having become conscious as black people relative to skin color and hair texture. When I first came to know of Frank, it was 1963, my first year at Jr. 1. James Brown hadn't sang "Say it Loud, I'm Black and I'm Proud" yet. We weren't sporting Afros or dashikis yet. After all it was '63 and the Black Thing hadn't happened yet but it was on its way although we couldn't have imagined it. Frank came from an intact well to do family and by appearances he seemed to have everything a child could want. He grew up on Race Street, right across the street from Jr. 1. He played basketball at the same school for a team called "Hoagland's Hero's." The team was deemed as such after its namesake coach Mr. Hoagland. At the time there was a television series on called Hogan's Heroes. The teams coached by Mr. Hoagland were city champs all of the three years I was at Jr. 1, the three years before I came and the three years after I left.

Frank as I remember it was the point guard on Jr. 1's squad. The starting five were Warren "Squirrel" Leveret, Clyde Duncan, Hayward McKenzie (father of Kareem McKenzie of the New York 2008, Super Bowl Championship team) and Frank Clark. This was an extraordinary young group of basketball players who totally dominated Junior High School Basketball in the city. They just couldn't be beat. I'm not sure that they ever lost. They also were innovators led by Frank's innovative mind. The basketball shoe or sneaker; Chuck Taylor Converse Allstars, was made of cloth. As history speaks, it was Frank who convinced the team to write their names and numbers on the side of their sneakers. It is believed by those of us who played ball and who lived in Trenton that not only were they the first innovators of athletic shoe logos in Trenton but they may have been the first in the country at least at the Junior High School level and there was no one at the High School level that was doing it at the time. It caught on like wildfire and may have had an influence on what we see today in athletic shoe brands from Nike to Adidas. Frank was also the back catcher for the school's baseball team. Having kneeled behind a plate or two, myself. Catching is one of the most difficult positions, if not the most difficult in baseball. And Frank Clark could catch – he was the absolute best. But where athletics are concerned Frank's claim to fame game was soccer. He was called "The Pollock!" Frank was a soccer God both at Jr. 1 and when it went on to play for Trenton Central High School.

But Frank was also a boy who was respected by his teachers, coaches and his peers. As much as I loved him as an athlete I loved him even more as a person. His shining moment in my memory is his fill in performance for another Boy on the list, Elsie Smith, aka "El Sid." Jr. 1 had an outstanding athletic department and outstanding physical education teachers one of whom was Ms. Downing. Ms. Downing was the teacher, trainer, choreographer and coach of the modern dance team.

The modern dance team at Jr. 1 was renowned for its modern dance program spearheaded by Ms. Downing, who by the way was "fine." She was absolutely gorgeous. Because we were seventh, eighth and ninth grade boys didn't stop us from noticing that she was. Anyway, Elsie was supposed to dance with Marietta Singletary, one of the finest girls in the school. For whatever reason, Elsie was a no show, dropped out or something and Frank had to fill in at the last moment. Boys, generally, weren't included in the modern dance program and no doubt would have been shunned by other boys if they had been allowed to. But this was a different story, this was Frank Clark and it also was a Fred Astaire moment or dance. Frank not only pulled it off but did it with grace and elegance. He looked like he had been ballroom dancing all of his life. When he dipped her toward the climax of the dance he convinced me forever that Frank Clark was a bad "mamma jamma," (in other words) if you know what I mean. The other thing that probably impressed me most about Frank was that he believed in reciprocity.

After he'd graduated he would come back to Jr. 1 and practice with our team. He was a mentor for us younger and less experienced soccer players and he graciously allowed us to play with the "Pollock." On one such occasion he yelled out, "Jordan is the only one hustling out here." It made my day to say the least, in as this testament speaks to, it was an everlasting event as I never forgot it.

The saddest account of my experience of Frank was in the last years of his life. I was living in New York at the time and had come back to Trenton for a visit of some sort. I ran into Frank on Broad Street near Perry Street. in front of where the old Garden movie house used to be.

During our conversation he revealed to me that he was HIV positive or moreover that he had AIDS or as referred to in Trenton, he had the "Package." He went on to reveal to me that he was not up on the Strip because he was being shunned by other guys who knew that he had the "Package." This was an amazing revelation to me in that all of the people that he was referring to were known to me and they had done, and were still doing the same thing that led to Frank being infected with the virus. Every one of them, was or is a long time heroin user just like nearly every boy on the list. The nerve of any of them to ostracize Frank like that on any day, any of them could be and some of them would be in the same boat.

When you talk about talent and especially athletic talent you would be talking about one of the best school boy athletes; while Trenton had many, you would be talking about Douglas Battle. Big Doug as we called him was an athletic specimen who had huge potential in almost every sport you could think of including basketball, track, football, baseball and diving. He was a phenomenal kid who could play almost anything at the highest level of the game. Doug came from a family of athletes which included three brothers Terry, Jackie and Michael. Together they represented one of the fastest relay foursome in track and field, they could all fly. The trophies at their home on Burton Avenue were too many to count and each of them in their own right was great.

"Mope" one of the Battle Brothers

I met Doug when we were both in the eighth grade at Jr. 1. Initially, we had some serious tension revolving around a girl that both of us liked a lot. Her name was Deborah Hall-Frails. She like a lot of the fine young girls of the day lived on Fountain Avenue. A life long friend of mine; another boy on the list, alerted me one day that Doug had put it out that he was going to beat me up. While this unnerved me it a bit, it wasn't because I was afraid of Doug although his size was a little intimidating, I was more concerned that he was in his neighborhood, as Jr. 1 was just a stone's throw away from Burton Avenue, where he lived. It was also the neighborhood of Warren "Squirrel" Levret, Rufus Watkins, Reggie Graves, Phillip Carpenter and a few others who lived in the same neighborhood, who might have his back. Long story short the fight never happened and I am glad it never did. While we grew up in an era when people who you fought against became your best friends, Doug and I became best friends without ever having to fight. Our friendship was

"Mope"

cemented by our having joined the school track team the same year.

As I said earlier, Doug was a phenomenal athlete. Imagine a 15 year old who could leap/jump over a bar 6'5" in the air. And also imagine that this is the outdoor season of the spring of 1965, three years before the "Fosbury Flop," a technique of high jumping invented by Dick Fosbury, who won the Gold Medal in the "68 Olympics jumping 7'4" and quarter inches. I am absolutely convinced that had Doug continued his involvement in track at the high school level and had he also mastered the Fosbury Flop, he would have bested Olympic athletes at the high school level. In fact, the same can be said for our entire track team. This might be hard for any of the readers to imagine but the boys from Jr. 1 at 15 years old were phenomenal athletes all around. Imagine having a 15 year old named Phillip Carpenter who could clock a 22 second 200 meters;

better known as the 220 Dash back in the day; a miler Johnny Vereen who was clocking just under four minutes; the mile, in what is now the 1500 meters.

We had cats like Stanley “Doc” Stroman, running the 100 meter high hurdles in under 15 seconds and boys like Rufus Watkins who ran a hundred yard dashes in 11 seconds. We had another miler on championship team, Gemes “MuscleHead” Wade, who never lost in our last year at Jr. 1. And then there was me, running what is now referred to as the 800 meters; back in the day it was the 880 Dash, best time in 2:01 minutes as a 15 year old, which by all accounts of coaches and college track meters that I ran against told me was phenomenal.

Our team won the City Track Championship the next two years. We also won at the New Jersey Jr. Chamber of Commerce Track and Field Meets two years running and Doug and myself never lost an event in the last year at Jr. 1. While these were nowhere near world record time, when you consider our ages and compare the world records of that day any of us were on pace to be world record holders and pound for pound we were. Doug and I would become the best of friends and I mean the best of friends.

We played together, sang together, drank together, got drunk together, smoked weed together and got locked up together, We got locked up at the “Poor People’s March” as it came through Trenton, New Jersey as it traveled through other North Eastern Cities on its way to Washington, D.C. Doug showed up at my parents home that day and he brought with him a fifth of Smirnoff Vodka, which we drank down until the bottle was empty. We then headed for the “Five Points” where we would meet up with others of our brud and the cast of characters which were sure to be present on a piece of land that we all called the “Strip.” The March would wind its way through the point turning on to North Warren Street right on the strip. After smoking marijuana or ‘reefer” or “smoke” as we used to call it and drinking wine, which included “Ripple” and “Bali Hai,”

You couldn't get any higher than we were. Our intoxication coupled with the energy of the day and the movement that was happening in America, lead by many of the Black Civil Rights leaders of the day, and the fact that Dr, King had been murdered and that our town was still recovering from the riot in Trenton as a result of Dr, King's assassination we were as determined to be a part of the March as we were drunk. We decided to get up on the back of a pickup truck filled with people and hay.

Doug grabbed onto the back of the truck as it was moving and I grabbed on to Doug. We were being told to get down or get back by one of the guys on the hay truck. He was guy we both knew and liked and he was a well known member of the boys who frequented the strip. While I don't want open old wounds, when Doug reached to pull himself up on the truck bed, he was pushed back by Isim back then he was known as Regis. It looked like he also kicked at Doug who was holding on to his pant leg, That's pretty much when all hell broke loose and the two of us went crazy.

"Big" Doug Battle

Long story short, we finally ended up in the hands of the police or should I say for me, back in the hands of the police. You see when they chased me down and put me in the back of the police paddy wagon, when I realized I was locked up I broke out while they were driving, I remember one of them shouting, "heeeeee's ooouuuuttt!!! I ran and but I was too drunk to get away and was caught, they lifted me up over their heads to take me back to the paddy wagon.

The Battle home on Burton Avenue was open to all of us. It was reminiscent of the Wade home when we were younger. You could come there and be there even when Doug, Jackie, Terry or Michael weren't at home. You were always welcome in Bet, their mother and Big Doug, Sr., their father's home. In fact it was at the Battle house that the STN's distributed our brand new club jackets, boy was that one of the proudest days of our lives, 40 young teenage boys who had raised enough money to buy 40 jackets and then to have 40 jackets embroidered was a supreme accomplishment for all of us. That next Monday at Trenton High, they thought the school had been invaded by boys wearing blue jackets. I remember being confronted at the second lunch period about having been at first lunch and I remember telling the cafeteria patrol guy that he should get ready because the blue jacket embroidered with STN would be at the third lunch again, "it's a lot of us man!"

I remember my Aunt Pauline was standing on the march route and saw me and hollered that's my nephew, let him down!! Well they didn't. I ended up in a captain's office a Chancery Lane, the location of the old police station. They were questioning me as if I were Rap Brown or somebody but soon stopped when all of the wine and vodka came crashing out of my mouth onto his desk and all over his papers, that's when they stopped the questioning.

Wow! The power of alcohol, and spent a night in the old Mercer County Jail on South Broad Street. The next day there was a full page spread in the local newspaper and Doug was the poster boy. They took a picture of him; that landed on the front page, being pulled back by Bucky Leggett, who was a community leader, organizer and activist and one of the people who was respected by a lot of us, on the Strip. Bucky, as he was affectionately called, played a central role in quieting the riot of 1968. We were also released the next day and were in school the same morning. Imagine that, being arrested, charged, and locked up in a matter of hours and detained in the county jail overnight, released the next morning and back in school on time for our 1st period class.

Many of the boys on this list were not just ordinary boys but they were Trenton's own. Some were boys of the great Cavalier's Drill Team, others sang to us as members of the "TNJ's" and "Instant Funk." In fact most of the boys that made up the TNJs had been members of the Cavalier Drill Team. Others like Don Roberson, Richard Nixon and

Greg Jamison and Scottie Miller: "Show Me The Money

Wayne Allen were "Master" barbers.

Wayne Allen: A Master Barber

Don Roberson was also a hustler in business for himself since childhood. He was my mother's paperboy, delivering the Trenton Times Newspaper. He was one of the few boys in North Trenton who rode a Schwinn bicycle with the big think tiers, fat leather seat and the big spring in the front. The only other boy in our area that I knew of was Ben Nixon who also rode one. Ben and his brother Larry recently buried their brother Bruce Nixon who transitioned this September, 2018. Don was also a race car driver, I

mean race car GTO at the track, "souped up" machines. He and another boy Eddie Richardson both h
drove powerful muscle cars of the day.

After his career as a paperboy he would hone his skills as a barber, first cutting hair out of his mother's apartment in the Downley Homes. He later began cutting hair at Miller's Barber Shop on Reservoir Street and as time passed he would eventually open up his own shop on Stuyvesant Avenue. Don was also a Golden Gloves Boxing Champion in the 147 lb weight class.

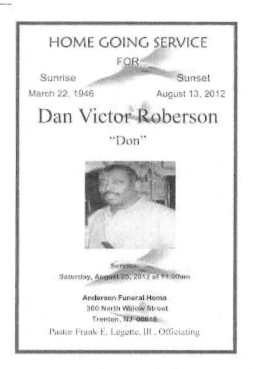

HOME GOING SERVICE

FOR

Sunrise Sunset

March 22, 1946 August 13, 2012

Dan Victor Roberson

"Don"

Service

Saturday, August 25, 2012 at 11:00am

Anderson Funeral Home

300 North Willow Street

Trenton, NJ 08618

Pastor Frank E. Legette, III , Officiating

Don like a lot of boys from Trenton could imo and he could also fight, he was a little guy but he fought big and never backed down, win, lose or draw in the ring or in the street. What a lot of people may not have known or remember about Don is that he was interested in, drove and raced fast cars and I mean fast cars.

There are other Golden Gloves Champions on the list including Rufus Watkins, John "Denny" Glover, Lee Grant Moses and a boy by the name of John Paul Lacey, who spent his life at the gym and was one of Trenton's very, very best amateur fighters. John Paul's downside in the ring is that he was in the same weight class as Sammy Goss. Sammy was a legend in the circles of Trenton boxing and he was both a mentor, sparring partner and nimesis of John Paul's as he beat him in the AAU finals every year for two or three years straight. Sadly, John Paul is one of the boys on the list who would be murdered.

There are boys on this list who, when you talk about *"Cool"* with a capital C you'd have to be talking about Stanley "Doc" Stroman, and Juan "Kopek" Perry and Lee Grant Moses. These are dudes who had what is called *"IT!"* These cats had a unique and special kind of swagger. And in terms of dressing I would put each of them in my top ten, in fact in my top five as its related to being three of the best dressed men I've ever met. While, for this writer, it was Bill Thompson, who set the standard and man, did he set the bar high; my God, he set it high. But of the younger boys like Doc and Kopek and Lee Grant these three would give all of us a run for our money.

While it was the clothes, it was also how they wore them, how they matched pieces, the quality of the "vines," the hats and the shoes. Nothing was ever out of place, with these three. They wore "vines" that awed you, set you aback, startled you, made you smile, made you acknowledge and pay homage. That's how tight it was and add to that their demeanor and flair, while subtle, matched the way they dressed, the way they talked and walked was consistent with the *"IT"* factor and all of them were handsome dudes.

Juan "Kopeck" Perry

Juan "Kopeck" Perry

Chapter Three: The Five Points: “The Strip”

The Five Points is a place located in North Trenton. It is distinguished or named such because of the coming together of five streets, Pennington Avenue, North Warren Street, Martin Luther King Boulevard, formerly named Princeton Avenue, Brunswick Avenue and North Broad Street. Its historic landmark is the “Battle Monument” a tall, small, Washington Monument looking building with a statue of George Washington ascending some one hundred and fifty feet into the sky. It stands to commemorate the “Battle of Trenton.” There is a small park at its base that runs south between Warren and Broad Streets. It was a place known for many things including some of the best food served in the city. Freddie’s Famous Steak House (cheesesteaks and hoagies) located on North Warren Street. Freddie’s was a household name especially for those of us who frequented the “Strip” and beyond.

The Shrimp Boat was located on Pennington Avenue and was owned and operated by the Kitchen family was also another eatery frequented by nearly everyone I knew at one time or another. There shrimp, fish, fish sandwiches, scallops, french fries would draw lines around the corner on Friday nights. It was seafood delight at the Shrimp Boat and always a joy when your parents brought home food from there.

Leroy Kitchen

The best breakfast was served across the Battle Monument Park at Willie Mitchell's restaurant on Broad Street. And if you wanted a drink you could find it in a few places, the C Bar which stood at the corner of Brunswick Avenue, the Monument Lounge which was located directly on the Strip on North Warren Street and the historic "Skippy Jake's" Liquor Store on Pennington Avenue just up from the Shrimp boat. So whether it was King Solomon, Chivas Regal, Twister, Hennessy, Swiss Up, Silver Satin,

Bacardi's Rum, Bali Hai, Courvoisier, Ripple, Boone's Farm Apple Wine, Yago Sangria, Champale, Miller Highlight, Colt 45, Orange Flip or whichever of the liquid spirits that your heart desired. These were institutions, which also included Sam's Hat Shop, The Hustler's Pool Room, The Shalamar Barbershop, Freddie's Famous Steak House, Brother Richard and Brother Danny's Steak and Take and the Drug Store on the corner, squeezed in between Pennington Avenue and Warren Streets where the two corners meet.

This small piece of earthen sidewalk we called the "Strip" was for everything it might not have been, it was a community and a democracy where the true hustlers gathered. It was a free marketplace that invited anyone who dared to visit. It didn't matter whether you were from North Trenton, East Trenton, Wilbur Section, West Trenton or South Trenton. In fact you could be from Hightstown, NJ or Ewing Township, NJ or Detroit, or Durham, Philadelphia, New York City, North or South Carolina or anywhere. If you were a hustler of any caliber you were welcomed on the Strip.

Without attempting to glorify anything that happened on the Strip or any of us who were apart of the fraternity and sorority of boys, girls, women and men who were apart of the daily cinema of happenings experienced by those who have come and gone including the writer, the Strip was a unique place in Trenton's history and while to many, it was an infamous Red Light District, to those of us who dared to frequent it every day it was a place of comic tragedy, where something was always happening, where goods were bought and sold, money won and lost, White Label, Chivas Regal, Hennessy, Gin and Tonic, Rum and Coke, King Solomon, Swiss Up, Orange Flip, Twister, Thunderbird, Bali Hai, Ripple, Boone's Farm Apple Wine, Manischewitz Cream White Concord, Morgan David's MD (aka: "Mad Dog 20-20) were drank and dope and coke, marijuana peddled, sniffed, shot and smoked, love and lust, whores and pimps, game and confidence schemes, shy larks or loan sharks, politics, police, redemption, murder, fine clothes and cheap wine, fine women and beautiful sissies. The things that we witnessed on this corner every day could have been a movie and could have competed with any of the so-called "blackSploitation" of the era; "Cotton Comes to Harlem;" "Car Wash; Across 110th Street;" "Superfly;" "The Mack;" "Watermelon Man," "Harlem Nights" or any of the others of the day.

This was the “Corner” that held a cast of characters with names like Fancy Max, Half Pint, Hard To Kill, Bronco, Junior Mason, Papoose, Charlie Jr., Goldie (Melvin), Snap, Mule Train, Pork Chop, the June Bugs; there were three June Bug’s, Church Rat, “Big Mug/Smash,” J.D. Ellis, Archie, Manzey, John and Ike Taylor, June Harvey, Trudell and Sister, Big Doug Posie, Catfish, Sammy Pack, Rambough, Pedro, Kopeck, Freddie Talarico (The Godfather), Big Bill Thompson, Cincinnati Kid, Kid, John Henry, Josh Mo, Happy, Hightstown, Bo Gant, Willingboro, Keith Hightstown, Dino, Little Rat, Rat, Left Hook, Po Bob, Freddie (Glove) Glover, Daniels, Tyrone “Juicy,” Rome, Mel, Ricky, June Harvey, Cleo, Jimmy “Stay Clean,” Big Twelve, Regis (Asim), Floyd, Lobo,

RING
LD
ST.

Dunlap

Dunlap, Jimmy Talarico, Head, Booty Bronson, Joe Vick, Little Vic, Otis/Philly, Regis, Bunky, Doc, Charlie Brown, Cool Jerry, Spook Juice, Chas, Andy Gump, Hook,Jesse Lee, Slim Oliver, Slim Jenkins, Stulu, Bostik, Felt, Fox, Bulu, Breezy, Brother Moon, Dinky, Charlie Bird, Sy Brown, Jimmy Stay Clean, Chill Will, Pete and Lucy,Big Rod and Bernice, Jerry Berry, Squirrel, Hollywood, Jesse Lee, Skippy Jake, Puddin, Reece, Eddie, Donald The Fox, Ms. Tot, Ms. Parkview and Erving, Ms. Tot, "Hot Cock Nell," Austin "Black" Pickett, Earl P, Sissy G, Sista "Matty/Big Debbie", Man, Scarlet, and many more.

Jim, Bulu, Charlie, Azim

Trenton: "The Town of Hats and Cadillacs"

(left to right) Catfish, Snap [top], Kopeck, Archie, Mel Smith, Big Doug Posey, Goldy

The Hustlers Pool Room was the premier gathering place for any and everyone who was a member of this fraternity of brothers. And for those of us who gambled in the corner's casino you would head to the back of the Shalamar Barbershop. We split cheesesteaks and cheese steak clubs, and hoagie sandwiches from Freddie's Famous Steak House.

Some of the boys who survived (pictured below) can attest to what is documented herein. I know it because as you can see it is a picture of smiles and we are not smiling just because we are taking a picture, we are smiling because it's been a long time since most of us have seen each other. We are smiling although we've come together for the "Home

Going Service" of one of our brothers; Eugene "Wimp" Woodson. We are smiling because we all know we have survived some very difficult challenges. We are smiling because we are Alive!

Trenton: *"The town of Hats and Cadillacs"*

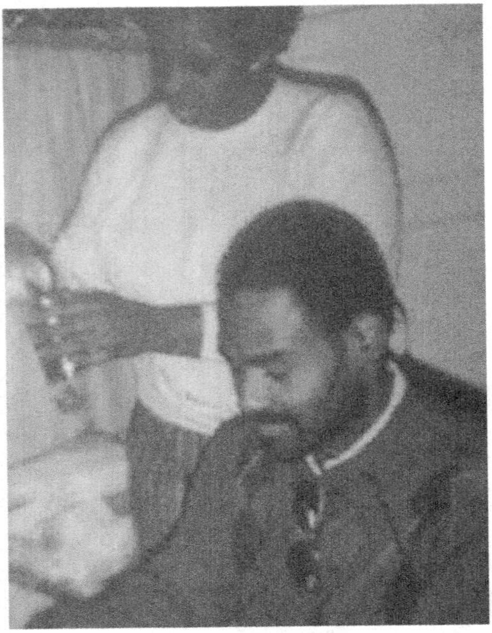

N. Warren St

The corner of North Warren and Pennington on the Strip!

Felton "Bruiser," Snooky Armstrong, Rome, Jesse Lee, Charles "Dino" (The Council)

trip: Pharmacy, Sam's Hat Shop to Danny & Richard's Steak & Take, Hustlers Pool Room, Shalamaar Barbershop, The Monument Lounge, Freddie's Famous Steak House, The Casino Residence at Rheingold, once upon a time at the 5 Points. Hallowed Ground!

CELEBRATING THE LIFE
of
SUNRISE
DECEMBER 16, 1951
SUNSET
NOVEMBER 14, 2013
Lee Grant
MOSES
Funeral Services
Thursday, November 21, 2013
11:00 am
New Life Christian Center
812 Prospect Street
Trenton, NJ 08618
Pastor Willie J. Granville, Pastor

The Boys at Wimp's Home Going Service

If you liked and/or loved street life the Strip was the place to be. If you wanted a career in hustling the Strip was the place where you could get a university education. In his book "Makes Me Wanna Holler," Nathan McCall talks about a place a lot like the Strip where he encountered the "first free black men I had ever seen." Well, I have strong identification with Nathan, when I read the piece in his book, I said wow! It was the same insight, the same premise that affected me when I came to the corner. I always knew what the Strip was about or at least so I thought

Alton, Bulu and Clarence (left to right) this photo was taken at the 5 Points in 2015, Alton Grier died in 2017.

Hallowed Ground

Horace Phelps

The Jones Brothers: Denny, David and Elijah

Eugene “Wimp” Woodson

Eli Woodson

A Celebration of Life for Our Beloved
Earthly
Entrance
"Eli"
Wayne Avenue Baptist Church

What I knew is that it was a place that was forbidden by my parents and if you went there for any reason other than to buy a cheese steak from Freddie's or fish from the Shrimp Boat; a Trenton institution, or to the movie at the Rialto or the occasional parade or that you were sent to the drug store, you shouldn't be caught by any older person or grown up. Older people where people older than me by three years or more they could pretty much tell you what to do. And you were forbidden on the Strip by real hustlers and players, they just didn't allow most kids to be on the Strip or partake in its daily regime of activities. But when they finally let me, I was impressed by these men. They wore the sharpest "vines." The clothes they wore were out of this world. They looked good, stood tall and spoke with conviction. One of the things that they said that I resonated to was, "I ain't gonna work nowhere for nobody." That's where the free black men thing came in for me.

Larry and David

They were talking about not working sure, but they were also talking about their respective independence and not having to be beholding to anyone else and especially not working a “slave” which was the term being used to describe a job. And although I only had a brief stint at pimping, when I heard one of them say that; “I don’t want no money but hoe money;” it put me on the floor. Wow, what kind of men are these? He said he didn’t want any other kind of money except hoe money. Statements like these impressed me immensely.

But there were other lessons to be learned, many more. Early on, one of the first lessons I learned was that "you got to know how to do something." This lesson would serve to be a valuable one. One of the hustlers on the corner was a cat by the name of Kid. Kid was a real player, southern dude, who talked with a southern draw, but he had all of the slick player features and he was smooth. He would always ask "how y'all 'gettin' long." I was on the corner one day and saw him, spoke to him and he replied in his usual. I'd just seen him fold up a decent "bank roll" of money and put it in his pocket. I stepped to him because I thought I'd gotten that familiar and asked him to borrow two dollars. Now mind you he'd just put in his pocket a bank roll that was clearly in the hundreds. In response he told me that he couldn't give me two dollars. He went on to say that if he gave me two dollars he would be making a bad hustler out of me. He also told me that if I was going to be on the Strip, I would need to learn how to do something. The latter is a theme that I would hear over and over again and one that I eventually took to heart and incorporated into a reputau of skills that where all outside of the law but skills that were very necessary to have on a place like the Strip.

(left to right) Slim Jenkins, Francis, Big Bill, BabyRoy, Tyrone, Andy Gump, Slim Oliver, James "Jitterbug," Thunderburg, Larry "Po Bob"

The Strip was a place of ill repute and illicit business enterprises which included a daily regime of illegal numbers game, a daily "crap" game in the back of Shalamar Barber Shop, marijuana, heroin, cocaine distribution and sales.

The Strip was also a place of commerce, including and with respect to almost every type of retail item sold in stores. You pretty much could buy and/or order anything that you wanted, from mink, leather, suede, rabbit, fox, tweed coats and jackets, to the best shirts, suits, jewelry, lamps, televisions, radios, music albums, steaks, and chops. Most of the items for sale where came to the Strip fresh out of the stores, new and in the box. Trudell and Sister "shopped" at Flemington Furs in Flemington, N.J., that sold some of the best fur coats in the region. Others of us "shopped" in downtown Trenton, New Hope, Pennsylvania, Peddler's Village, The Oxford Valley Mall; in fact we opened the Oxford Valley Mall, EJ Korvettes, the Independence Mall in Trenton and throughout Bucks

County Pennsylvania and New York City. We even boosted out of well known establishments like Charlie Byers, The Shirt Shop, Havenson's, Rauch's Coats, even when they knew us by name and like Charlie Byers who knew my mother and her name. We stole even when the sales people like Danny and Earl knew us and also knew that we came to steal. What can I tell you we loved money and we loved to dress!

LeeRoy and Lee

Johnny Baker and Tyrone George at the 5 Points

"Just trying to make some noise, for US and the Boys", At The 5 Points

The "Strip" probably had one of the best collection of "boosters" (shoplifters/thieves) in the nation. This is said not to glorify or gloat about wrongdoing but it is to tell the truth from my personal perspective. And if another truth be told a lot of hard working, honest people who lots of times were in possession of the stolen property that was purchased by them from these thieves including "yours truly." This is said not to tell on the good folks but rather to give the reader insight as to how this community, however illicit, thrived as a business entity.

“DIAMOND JIM WILCOX” (Then)

Jim Wilcox (Now)

Jim, Lindsey and Larry

Clarence, Larry, Ben

Burying The Dead Again: Photo Scene at Hughes Funeral Home Bellevue Avenue

The former retail goods were sold to ladies who got their hair done at Fox's shop on Princeton Avenue (Martin Luther King Blvd.), many of them church going Christian women. Goods were sold to bar patrons from the Monument Lounge on the Strip to the C Bar at the corner of Brunswick Avenue along the turn at North Broad Street to the Turf Club also located on Princeton Avenue (aka MLK Blvd). Much of the "weed" sold on the Strip was sold to hard working everyday people who wanted to puff an occasional marijuana joint or a toke of coke or a blow of dope from time to time. The illegal wine and whiskey that was sold on Sunday to many of the good folk was supplied to the middleman; Uncle Yulie, who sold it, came from the legitimate "Skippy Jake's Liquor Store" on Pennington Avenue, a Five Point institution. Skippy Jake, a white Italian guy was into a lot of shit, including the number rackets and he was a fence who bought stolen jewelry especially diamonds. The business enterprises on the Strip could not have prospered without so called "Squares," the good legal people. Uncle Yulie Mason was that middle man, a middle man and an illicit entrepreneur on several levels who outlived all of the boys on the list having died in his early eighties.

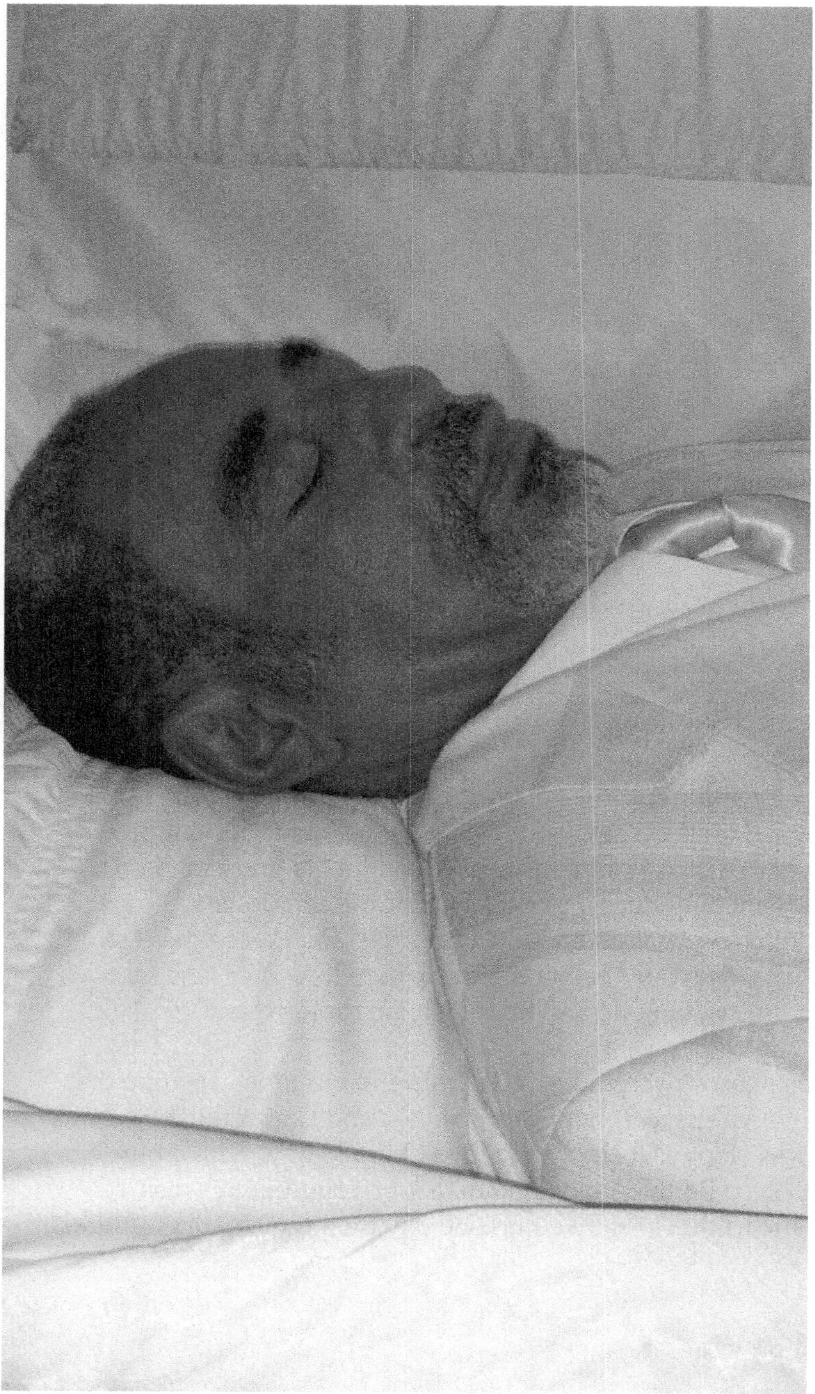

Charlie Jr., PoBob, BabyKong

While there were gambling spots all over Trenton, the epicenter of gambling happened on the Strip. There were days and nights that there could be better than a quarter of a million dollars in the house and on a real good night there could be as much as a half million dollars. Thousands of dollars were won and lost every day and those who lost hundreds or thousands would be back the next day to win or lose all over again. We called it 'backing up and betting again tomorrow."

There were even showdown crap games, from time to time. The one that stands out in my memory was between Josh Mo and Happy. Josh Mo was a pimp and so was Happy. Josh, a little light skinned guy, with a big voice, meaning he could talk loud and talk a lot of shit but he wasn't plastic, he was the truth. He showed up one day on the Strip in a Cadillac

Fleetwood filled to the brim with hoes that looked like they were from every nationality and every color under the rainbow. The car was muddy from back to front appearing as if it had been driven across a muddy swamp. I remember him getting out of the car and shouting out, asking Happy to "Come Outside and See What A Real Pimp Looks Like." When he finally went in he kicked the front door and broke it off the hinges. The Crap-House had moved from the back of the barbershop in the middle of the block to the building at the corner of Warren and Rheingold Streets.

The crap game (dice) was already underway when Josh went in but it soon turned into a duel between Josh and Happy. Josh was shooting the dice and caught a 10 or a 4 for his number. Ten and four bets for a right better gets two to one odds in the right betters favor. Josh put down a small stake of money, on the top of which was a $100 dollar bill. When he "cut the number in," (made it) he slide the bills to spread them out vertically. The first two bills were $100 bills but the next twenty were $1000 dollar bills, which means Happy had to

Lee Grant, Andy, LeeRoy, Tyrone

Juan "Kopeck" Perry

Baker, Picket, Andy, Erving & Richard (left to right)

Larry "Po Bob" Housley

Alton, Bulu, Clarence

come up with. $40,200.00.

I remember Josh asking him, “can you pay that Nigga, wit yo good pimping self? Happy, didn’t blink, he threw his car keys to Big Doug Posie and told him to go to the truck of his car. Doug came back with a silver box and Happy opened it and paid off the bet and the game proceeded. This was the kind of high drama that went on daily on the Strip and it’s what we came back to be a part of everyday.

Nearly every day you would hear someone cry out “Lord Send Rain,” or it’s “Hard But It’s Fair.” When we thought that someone may be an undercover cop, a snitch, a police officer or just someone who we thought should not be in the know, or a stranger, you would hear cries like “phone of the hook,” and/or “strange weed in the garden.” What we didn’t know was that a lot of us would die early and that being on the Strip as a participant of its daily affairs would be a nexus; a connection, to these early deaths in one way or another. See if you were involved in any kind of illegal activity, if you consider yourself a hustler, a player, a money getter, no matter what part of town you were from or where your primary center of hustling might have been, at some point you had to visit the Strip. This was the case whether you were picking up money, dropping it off, picking up a product/work, selling or picking up or paying off a numbers hit, gambling in the crap house or just having a drinks with friends, you stopped off at the Five Points. I am almost certain that not one of the the two hundred boys remembered herein and those of us who have survived visited and spent time on the Five Points during our lifetimes.

Charlie Jr., Andy Gump. Sultan (aka: Donny Ray), Isim (aka: Regis Gates), Boolou Johnson, LeeRoy "BabyRoy" Jordan, Eugene "Breezy" Briggs

Chapter Four: The Pied Piper Cometh: When Heroin Was King

If there is any single reason that stands out to account for the deaths of the overwhelming majority of the boys it lies in a single source. Almost every death, either directly or indirectly, can be linked to a period in the late 1960's throughout the 1970's until the middle 1980's, when heroin became King. Ninety of the boys who represent over sixty percent had a history of heroin use, abuse and/or addiction. They, like the writer, were all young men who came out to dance to the tune of the Pied Piper of Heroin. Like the rats that followed the pied piper of the famed fairy tail we would; like the rats of the tale, dance our way into a river of despair, pain, disease, deprivation and for many of us, death associated with the powerful lure and addiction to this drug.

The number of casualties is a horrific epithet of what happened to us as a result of our following the tune of the Pied Piper of Heroin. This drug took the lives of many of us by overdose, homicide, and HIV/AIDS in the prime of our lives. And for those of us that it didn't kill outright, it drug us through the muck and mire of torment that left us with irreparable scars, jail and prison terms, methadone programs, inpatient rehabs and therapeutic communities, hospitals, homelessness, family estrangement, loss of all dignity and self-respect and more. We lost our minds, our hearts, our spirits and our morals. We lost everything that we grew up with, the values given to us by our parents, teachers, coaches, ministers and mentors. This drug had a devastating impact on our city that can be felt and witnessed to this day, leaving its signature across three generations of Trentonian.

Oftentimes in the world of drug addiction lore there are many true stories of young people who became addicts whose parents were addicts or who grew up in horrible and blighted neighborhoods and dysfunctional parents and poverty and other social ills. But when I think about the lives of many of those of us who grew up in Trenton including the overwhelming majority of the boys on the list, we and including many children who to my knowledge who never touched drugs; for the most part, don't have those kind of stories. In fact if the truth be told, most of us grew up in working class, blue collar and middle class homes. We grew up in a time when most African American fathers were heads of were still at home.

There were children who I grew up with whose parents were teachers, ministers, police officers, and doctors. "Squeeter" Woodson was the son of Mrs. Woodson who was my second grade teacher, who was the wife of Howard S. Woodson, Sr. the long time Pastor of Shiloh Baptist Church who was one of the most powerful and influential people in the entire state of New Jersey. One of the boys not on the list but known to me to use heroin is the son of two teachers both of whose classes many of us were in during our junior high school and high school experience. Quinton "Quinny" Smith was the son of Quinton "Smitty" Smith; who did not use drugs to my knowledge, a Trenton police officer who lived next door to my aunt on Humbolt Street. Two of the boys I grew up with are the sons of a preacher who was the Pastor of Union Baptist Church where my mother took me as an infant and did all she could to keep me there. A lot of the boys from Prospect Village and the Campbell/Frazier Homes, particularly the McNeil brothers, attended Union Baptist Church and those who didn't attend the Carver Center YMCA Summer Day Camp.

Many of our parents worked at any number of the manufactures mentioned earlier during a part of Trenton's manufacturing hay day. To my knowledge, with a single exception, none of the people I just mentioned ever used heroin but they are a small sample of who our parents were and what our community looked like and who lived there. We grew up in a time when African American doctors (Dr. Shepard and Dr. Frazier) still lived, had offices and practiced in the African American community and Mr. and Mrs. Turner owned a grocery store and a live poultry market on Reservoir and Frazier Streets and Mr. and Mrs. Glover owned a variety store that sold the best candy in the world on Willow Street.

The heroin plague consumed the lives of the best and the brightest of us, stealing in some cases, every child in the family. The forty-one clusters of brothers that help to make up the list of the dead Boys of My Summers, to a boy/man were killed by this plague either directly or indirectly. Heroin changed everything. Some of the coolest, smartest, slickest, handsome, talented, educated, brightest young men, who had enormous potential and whose parent's socioeconomic status was in the middle class range would succumb to the scourge of drug dependence. While there were "old timers" or "old heads" who had been using heroin for longer than any of the boys had lived yet they came few and far between. Heroin, historically, in the black community was a secret and this was true throughout the country. Not everybody was qualified to buy heroin nor did most people know where to buy it. An old timer once told me that he remembered when the police didn't know what heroin was. He said he'd been stopped by the police on numerous occasions and they would toss the heroin aside still looking for whatever they were looking for ignorant of the fact that he was in possession of a controlled narcotic drug. But by 1968 this would all change.

Any number of the guys that I'd looked up to, were changing. Right before our eyes there was a metamorphosis happening but I was just a little too naive to fully appreciate what was happening and I certainly had no clue as to what was going to happen when the King took hold. Now they were still clean, still fly, still sharp and all of them were "in with the in crowd." They were still wearing gators and Bly Shop shirts, silk and mohair slacks, diamond cluster pinkies, and the best cuts. Their pockets still had the "mumps." Your pockets had the mumps back then when they were full of cash, a large bank roll that stuck out of a pocket and sometimes two pockets for all to see. However, they were beginning to fall asleep or so it seemed. Their lips were turning red from the sweet sodas they were drinking and they were beginning to scratch and had a gray ashen look to them. At first the change was subtle. But by the next year, 1969, it was real clear that many of the boys including any number of them who were my heroes were marching to the tune of the Pied Piper of Heroin. This drug changed everything. It changed the way that we walked, talked, what we did, how we did it, what we cared about, and what we would do, to get this drug.

In the 1940's, '50's and 60's it was said the Post Office was the graveyard for black talent. Well in the late 1960's and early 1970's Heroin addiction would become the graveyard for black talent in our town. Literally, hundreds of boys, young men and some of the most beautiful, smart, intelligent, talented young girls and women would succumb to the music of the Piper.

Marsha Travers

I don't think you can find any of us who are still alive who would tell you that they had any idea of what was about to happen to us that dared to enter into this arena. We had absolutely no clue as to how this thing would end up, none whatever. It would make us turn on each other. It turned some of us into police informants "snitches" that would tell on his mama. It made some of us temporarily rich but it also took its toll by the number of untold years that many of us spent in jails and prison. For those who frequented the Strip there were few who escaped its clutches and its wrath.

It would be the central causal factor for what resulted in the murder of some of us and it would drive the rest of us crazy. It would have some of us commit both intentional and unintentional suicide. It would have a brother kill his sibling. Cliffy Armstrong would die at the hands of his younger brother indirectly as a result of his using. It would have a guy like John Paul Lacey, who was never a gangster, or stick up guy, rob one of our own and it would almost immediately cost him his life. It would have Vernon Bond commit a robbery inside of the C Bar on the Five Points only to come outside and stick the shot gun he was welding down into his front pants with his hand still on the trigger, accidentally having the gun discharge and taking his life. It would have my beloved cousin Billy Sanders hang himself in the newly built police headquarters at Clinton Avenue. It would have Scoffield Patterson and Linda Housley, disappear while, reportedly, living in New York, and Scoffield never to be found.

Heroin would kill Milton Tucker, Jeffrey Goss, George “Kobo” Locket, Earl “Brother Moon” Thomas, Gregory Jamison, Melvin Smith, Elsie “El Sid” Smith, Dale and David Fitzgerald, Kenneth “Mule Train” Bethea, Levi “Tony” Blackwell, Donald Clark, Karl Teape and more recently Hampton Jenks; in 2018, by way of a lethal overdose, respectively. I’d be remiss not to mention the overdose/heroin poisoning of Marcia Travers. Marcia aka Marsha was 19 years old when she died in 1972 and of this writing she has been gone for 46 years, nearly half a century ago. Simply put there is no other phenomena that has outright taken so many lives whether directly or indirectly as did heroin. Most of these deaths came before 1975 BC (Before Crack) the advent of the Crack Cocaine epidemic which began in the mid 1980’s, as aforementioned regarding the death of Marcia Travers.

If you lived during this era it would be filled with the twist and turns of drama, from “Little Pete's Tighten Ups;” to the sudden and out of nowhere arrest orchestrated by Big Ronald Sapp a trenton Narcotics Police officer, to the murder of James “Handsome” Ransom, to the Boston exodus of scores of people who were named in secret indictments related to selling heroin, to the stick up boys like Fox, Willie, Junie, Burley who if you sold heroin were extremely dangerous. The “Tighten Ups” thrown by Little Pete were what you would call “Dope” aka heroin, dope shooting parties held at a location and Pete would give away dope and people who used would tighten up. The latter was a pretty brilliant marketing strategy as a means to sell a lot of dope by giving it away before putting it on the street.

Then there were the lives lost to heroin poisoning aka overdoses, one of the earliest being Brother Moon Thomas, home less than 72 hours after having been released from Bordentown after serving a prison bid, who died inside of the stairwell in the Lincoln Homes in 1971, 47 years ago and again nearly half a century. Another earlier death was that of George "Kobo" Lockett, there was also Milton Tucker, Jeffrey Goss, Marsha Travers, the Fitzgerald twins, Dale and David, Kenneth "Mule Train" Bethea, and later Louise Berry, Gregory Jamison, Donald Clark, Elsie Smith, Mel Smith and the murder of John Paul Lacey, the unintentional self inflicted shotgun blast that killed Vernon Bond as he exited the C Bar at the 5 Points, after he had completed a drug robbery.

The shear devastation and the death rate of those written about herein and the city to which they belonged is unprecedented. The link between heroin addiction, intravenous use of the drug as the route of administration and HIV/AIDS is an established fact that caused the deaths of many of the boys on the list. In fact most of those who were not overdose or homicide victims were victims of the virus that Trentonian"s called "The Package." And the siege has not stopped. As recent as August, 2018, reportedly, Hampton Jenks, like most of the boys was a lifelong from childhood friend, die at nearly sixty-eight years of age. And while heroin killed any number of us directly or indirectly, it was "WET" the Dust, PCP, Angel Dust that killed Jackie Walker.

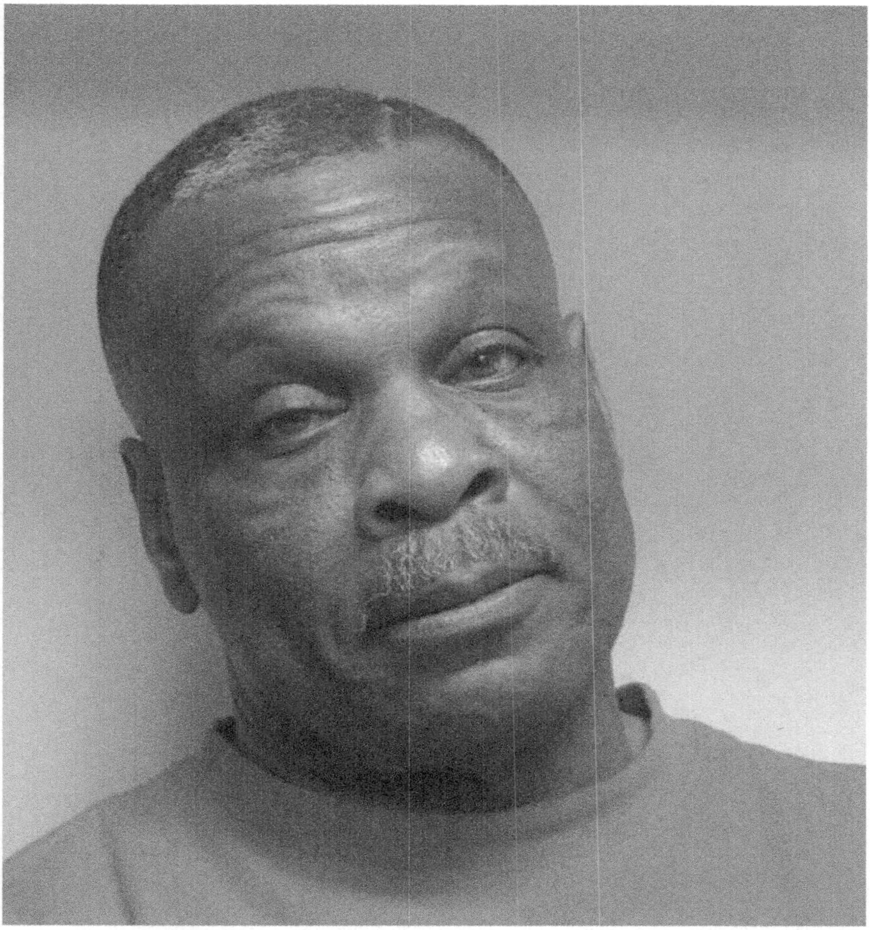
Hampton "Hamp" Jenks

Jeffrey Goss

One of the earliest to die of a heroin drug overdose was "Brother Moon," who was one of the Thomas brothers from Prospect Village. Brother Moon's death was an earth shaking event on the strip. He died about 48 hours after he had come home from Bordentown Reformatory. He died in a hallway in one of the buildings in the Lincoln Homes at Old Rose Street. He would be the first of four Thomas brothers to die either directly or indirectly as a result of the heroin scourge but he wouldn't be the last. Moon's death shook up the strip, not only because he'd just come home but also because he was renowned, respected, a leader, a player, a role model and straight cool! But his death would also leave a bad taste in the mouth of those of us who frequented the Strip, especially his brothers. We'd learned that some of the folks who we all knew; one in particular, was with him on the night that he died. And if the historical reports are to be held as true, Moon was left that night by a guy who also was held in high esteem and known to almost everyone on the Strip. These revelations would change the feelings of many of the boys toward this guy forever. While he was still accepted on the corner; to a degree, he was never really trusted by anybody after that night when for all intent and purpose, he left Brother Moon to die and die he did.

Dale and David Fitzgerald were identical twins who were about five years my junior. Around 1979 I was living in New York City in the Bronx. As would happen from time to time folks from Trenton would come to New York to take care of their business as far as buying and in some cases also using the drugs they purchased. On one of these occasions Big Doug Battle and Little Sonny, two guys I hadn't seen in years. In fact I was surprised as hell to learn that Doug used dope. This was something that he vehemently opposed but things change and there were a lot of us who it happened to. While at my house I asked Sonny what had been happening with him. His response was like "you haven't heard?" Heard what, I asked? He went on to tell me that he'd just gotten out of jail after two years. He said that the Fitzgerald twins had both died in his house. Died of what, I asked?

They “ODed” he said! Both of them? Yea! Sonny went on to tell me that they had bought heroin that morning and went to his house. He said his wife was at work and they all got high together. He said that they went out to cop again and while doing so the two of them were drinking beer and arguing and fighting like they always did. He said when they got back to the house they all shot some more dope and proceeded thereafter to nod out, one of the effects of the drug.

Sonny said, “I woke up again and looked over at the couch where they were both sitting and they both were nodded out with their heads leaning on each other, I didn’t think nothing of it and I nodded out again but when I came out of it they were still in the same position. I went over and shook both of them and one of them fell over. I said to myself, now I know that you two mother……….s ain’t dead so I shook them some more and I kept on shaking them but they wouldn’t wake up. My wife was at work and would be coming home soon and I didn’t know what to do and was about to lose my mind and finally I decided to call the police, wasn’t nothing else I could do. The police wanted to know why I was still alive if we shot the same thing but I didn’t know, but the only thing that I didn’t do that they did was drink, but that’s what happened and I only been out about a week.”

Over and again I hear about the unavailability of African American men because of how many of us are incapacitated by incarceration in America's jails and prisons. But if the truth be told the primary reason that there are not enough of us, that we are unavailable, that we are not with our families and being fathers to our children is not because we are in jails and prisons. Men in jails and prisons are available. Go to any prison or any jail visiting center and see how many people in particular women and children who are there to visit them. In fact there are countless numbers of African American men who get married and even father children while in prison and to the best of their ability parent their children from behind prison walls. The reason that all of the children of the Boys of My Summers went fatherless is because their fathers were permanently unavailable because of the pathology of excess and premature death. Excess and premature death is a primary if not the primary cause of so many black women and children being on there own and alone and without the men they loved as father, husbands, lovers, significant others and friends.

When I look back on the heroin epidemic of Trenton I remember that before heroin there was another drug epidemic among young boys in our early teens (13,14 years of age) and in Jr. High School. It was the glue epidemic of the early 1960's. Young black boys had discovered the inhalant glue could alter our state of consciousness. While I wasn't a chronic glue sniffer, I certainly tried it and more than once. And I also went to buy it a few times. We could and would buy glue from the "Hobby Shop" on East State Street. Glue sniffers from all over town new you could buy glue a the Hobby Shop. Thus if there is a so-called 'stepping stone" drug for many of the boys who eventually used heroin, it wasn't marijuana, it was Glue!

The opioid/heroin epidemic that has become the current day contemporary scurge of America had visited itself on black people in this country; like it did in Trenton; years ago, four plus decades ago. And we paid a much higher price, jails, institutions and DEATH! In fact what we have learned since is that our own government launched a campaign to destroy black lives and black communities as it looked away while supporting the heroin trade as it flooded the black community.

"You understand what I'm saying? We knew we couldn't make it illegal to be either against the war or black (i.e., black people) but getting the public to associate the hippies with marijuana and blacks with heroin. And then criminalizing both heavily we could disrupt those communities, Ehrlichman said, we could arrest their leaders, raid their homes, break up their meetings and vilify them night after night on the evening news. Did we know we were lying about the drugs? Of course we did."

Straight Outta The White House, the truth about how a President (Nixon) helped to collude to destroy the black community through the heroin trade industry and then both lock up and kill black people who bought, sold and used the drug in mass, therefore literally destroying black communities throughout America and Trenton was one of those places.

As reported by CNN's "one of Richard Nixon's top advisors, John Ehrlichman of Watergate infamy said "the war on drugs was created as a political tool to fight blacks and hippies, according to a 22-year old interview recently published by Harper's Magazine. The Nixon campaign in 1968, and the Nixon White House after that, had two enemies; the antiwar left and black people." The Pied Piper SIngs and he Danced!!!

Some Trentionians believe that it was the "riot" of 1968 that started the decline of Trenton as we once knew it is a premise that is partially true, however, there is a profound correlation and nexus to the opioid/heroin plague that began to stain the fabric of our city like it would cities big and small throughout the country and the Nixon administration's so-called war on drugs which was actually a war on black people and our communities as much as the riot of Trenton and scores of other cities had its nexus to the assassination of the Reverend Dr. Martin Luther King and the oppression, discrimination, brutality and murder of black people and the destruction and intentional dismantling of our cities which continues to prevail to this very day, Dr. King said that "riots are the voice of the unheard."

LeeRoy “BabyRoy” Jordan, 17 years Old/STN

The Trentonian

WILD LOOTING, FIRES JAR CITY

Youth Is Killed During Outbreak

A City Gone Mad

Night to Be Frightened

Violence, Fires, Lootings Rip City

The Evening Times

LATE FINAL EDITION

Trenton, N. J., Wednesday, April 10, 1968

Ten Cents

City Wary After Night Of Terror

City-Wide Curfew Is Reimposed By Mayor

Many Areas Sealed

Summer Came Early

Flames … Gunshots … Taunting Laughter

'Cool It' Teams Out To Help

Youth Slain; 108 Arrested

Convery's North Broad Street furniture store wantonly destroyed

The Trenton riot while brewing for days after the April 4, 1968 murder of Dr. King boiled over on Tuesday, April 9, 1968 in earnest. In fact the first serious outbreaks of violence didn't start in downtown Trenton or the 5 Points, the first serious outbreak began at Trenton Central High school and it was mostly young boys who deboarded the buses from Trenton High, that stopped in downtown Trenton who began the first rattling of the cage of chaos that would eventually become contagious. From our side of town, North Trenton at the 5 Points on The Strip, I should know because I was there! There was a growing tension on the Strip all afternoon. I was one of the high school aged young people who had arrived on the Strip after school, having deboarded the bus at State and

Broad in downtown Trenton, a downtown that would be transformed and changed forever before the night was over.

The tension on the Strip was visible and its volume was growing louder by the minute. It's approximately 6:30 p.m. While standing on the north corner of Warren Street between Sam's Hat Shop and the corner Drug Store one of the boys on the list; Erving Jackson, picked up a shiny metal garbage can and lifted it to throw into the window of Sam's. Sam's Hat Shop is was institution and there is probably nobody I know who lived anywhere near the 5 Points who had not bought a hat, cap, a shoe or shirt from Sam's and Sam himself was beloved. Someone shouted out to Eriving, "hey Eriving that's Sam's man!!" Erving complied in sort and lowered the can and brought it back to the ground, but in a millisecond, he lifted the can and said "fuck Sam" and threw the can through the window and the riot and looting began. We moved from Sam"s to Skippy Jake's liquor store and where we were met at the entrance by Skippy Jake holding a shotgun, sensible, we backed off and turned to move across the park, some of us to Convery's Furniture store and a larger group headed down Broad Street to downtown Trenton.

The first store the group I was in hit was Havenson's Mens clothing, the best money can buy. It's where George Dash's; one of the boys on the list, night would end, after a large chuck of the plate glass window would fall on him leaving a horrible looking gash in his head. My night would end hours later by being arrested (see picture above) on broad Street in front of the old red "Junkie 5 and 10 Cents Store across from Simmon's Mens Store.

There were hundreds of people arrested that night including scores of juveniles, which I was one of. I'd catch up with George later that night at Chancery Lane; the Police Station, after I was able to open my eyes from the excruciating burning pain of the pepper spray administered during my arrest. The picture above doesn't reflect what happen next and what happen is I broke loose and fought as hard as I could, they swung blackjacks or nightsticks mostly hitting each other. Finally one of them grabbed my hair from behind and pulled my head back and sprayed me in my eyes, I thought they'd blinded me, it was extremely painful however even blinded I was like a wild bull and my last visual was Big Smitty; Quinton Smith, Sr., one of Trenton's first Black Police Officers. He lived next door to my Aunt Pauline on Humboldt Street, I grabbed onto him in my blindness, screaming, hurting, outraged and pulled him or he let me pull him into the paddywagon as he tried to calm me and convince me that I was not permanently blind.

(back row l-r) Quntillious Smith, Robert O'neal, Johnie W. Sapp, Lester Young, William Winston, John Purdy, (front row l-r) Lone Hodges, Ronald W. Hortenberry, Marvin Holmes, Theopolius Baker, Leon smith (June 23, 1957)

Later at the police station, when I opened my eyes, George who's night had ended at the outset was sitting across from me. His eyes were the most bloodshot eyes that I had ever seen in my life and I remember asking him what happen to his eyes and he said, "the same thing that happened to yours! George had been sprayed too, it's kinda humorous now thinking about it after all these years but not that night. I thought if my eyes looked like George's and he'd assured me that they did then we'd been permanently injured for life!

After first being booked as an adult when asked my date of birth and they realized that I was a juvenile, which angered them and I was threatened with physical violence if I was found to be lying to them. I was appropriately booked as a juvenile and sent off to spend the next thirty six hours on the third floor of the old Mercer County Jail on South Broad Street with all the other juveniles locked up that night. This was my first time being locked up overnight. I was even more enraged that ever, pulling on the bars, literally trying squeeze my head through, which was itself insane. It was Johnny Coles; a juvenile veteran of this madness, who was locked next to me said, "Roy just lay down, you we can't get out of here until they let us out."

Youth, 19, Who Was Killed Active In City Teen Councils

By THOMAS H. GREER
Staff Writer

The youth who died in last night's rioting was a 10-year-old college student who was killed while allegedly fleeing a looted downtown clothing store.

Harlan B. Joseph, a sophomore at Lincoln University, Oxford, Pa., died at 7:58 p.m. in Helene Fuld Hospital of bullet wounds in the lower back.

A police officer fired the shot which killed Joseph, marking the first major incident of the riot.

Joseph, of 49 Carroll Street, was a religion major at the Pennsylvania University. He also was interested in social work.

Cite Evidence

Evidence indicated Joseph was one of the looters, police said. Merchandise from Charm-Aronson Inc., 382 East State Street, was scattered ner his body.

However, police had not determined today whether Joseph was one of the plunder-

(Continued on Page 2, Col. 8)

HARLAN B. JOSEPH
... dies in rioting.

On Thursday, April 11, 1968 the parents of all juveniles were summoned to be at the back entrance of the Mercer County Jail at 2:00 p.m. at which time all of us would be released into their custody. I remember getting home and my mother showing me that my picture was in the paper. I was being held on each side by police officers, my STN jacket; my pride, blazing in the what felt like a hot humid summer night except it was April yet the night felt like a scalding July 4th filled with the chaos of sirens, police, screams, shattering glass, snatching, grabbing, fighting, pushing, shoving, smoke, the ratched smell of pepper spray in our nostrils and in my case in my eyes.

After the 1968 Riot talking with Mayor Armenti and Bo Robinson

However, after the Trenton Riot there was no court proceedings for any of the juveniles and while any number of older guys who I knew and recognized coming into the precinct that night I have no memory of anyone being sentenced to jail or prison for any of the acts that occurred that night. What I do remember is the carnage and the cost, the overcrowded police precinct, overcrowded county jail and the mayhem that cost Trenton its life as we knew it and the city's heroin scourge would continue unabated erasing the dreams and possibilities that includes literally taking too many of our lives. And even though they demolished the buildings that lined the Strip the finger and footprints of the Good, Bad and the Ugly that happened there and its memories will never be erased until we are all dead!

Most of the written history of the riot of Trenton either ignores or gives little to no account of the role of the beginning of the full blown city "rebellion" that actually began at Trenton High School, where the first origins of violence occurred and would move into downtown Trenton after students deboarded buses later in the afternoon and would eventually become a full scale riot; as aforementioned, later in the evening. We were the first to experience the chaos and violence both as victims and victimizers.

Reverend Dr. Howard S. Woodson % Honorable Albert "Bo" Robinson

Chapter Five: Second To None "(STN)": Not A Fraternity, But We "Coulda" Been

Second To None (STN) were a group of teenage boys comprising thirty-five members from every part of the City. Some of us had known each other from the time we were in elementary school, others of us met when we were in junior high school and the rest us came together when we met and fell in love with each other in high school. The group came together around 1967 when most of us were about 16. The eldest of the group was Karl Teape, who was named as our first and only President. Karl was given the distinction simply because he was one of the two oldest member; the other Ernest "Little Geech" Scott, the Vice President, back then if you were older, this was respected.

Karl Teape

There were forty of us. Other members of the club were Wayne Allen, Clifford Armstrong, Johnny “Bake” Baker, Doug “Big Doug” Battle, John “Bo” Bethea, Eugene “Breezy” Briggs, William Brown aka (Ramadan Salahuddin), Reese Byrd, William “Baby Kong” Clark, Johnny Coles, James Cooks, Furman Counts, Arthur “Squeak” Duncan, Henry “Bro/Slim Jenkins” Ellison, Charles “Eddie” Franklin, Jimmy Glover, Melvin Hopps, Kenneth “Country” Griffin, Larry “Po Bob” Housley, LeeRoy “BabyRoy” Jordan, Freddie Little, Stanley “Tank” Loman,Bob McCrea, Arthur McCrea, James “Bubby” McKenzie, Xavier “XMO”Moore, Lee Grant Moses, Garland Murray, Lindsey “Butch/Monster” Page, Melvin Douglas “Pic” Pickett, Donny (Sultan) Ray, Ernest “Little Geech” Scott, Johnny “Little Geech” Scott, Barry Stewart, Sam Ward, Charles Gerald “Dinky” Warren, Alfred “ Little Alfred” Williams, Rayfield Woody.

BabyRoy, Country, Breezy

We were a Club, a Social Club and we were the best, baddest, brightest, fun, most popular club of any group of teenage boys in the history of Trenton, New Jersey, we were party children. Our parties where renowned including the first ever STN Christmas Extravaganza thrown at the old St. Paul's AME Zion Church formerly located at 308 North Willow Street; now located in Ewing Township. Being the respectful children that we were, we didn't sell or drink any wine in the church, although while the night was not about Communion wine may have been appropriate. However, we did have a rum punch that was made for us by one of our mothers and it was a respectful drink and we were a respectful group of young people.

While we didn't tell the Church mothers and fathers that we were going to be doing a little drinking, we appreciated the fact that they trusted us enough and that it may have been the only time in the history of Trenton and its black churches that a church let a group of young men come into a place of divinity to have a party!

St. Paul AME Zion Church-Willow Street

And the biggest ever bash we threw was at the old Pittsburgh Glass Company building located at the tip of North Broad Street where it met with Brunswick Avenue. The way we made our money was through throwing house parties. Some of our mothers were insane enough and brave enough to allow us to have a party in their homes and amazingly nearly all of them were a success, big time! Shit, we threw a "Waist Party" in the Campbell Homes, aka, the Frazier Homes at Garland Murray's house, or should I say his mother's house and we made over $300 that night. We measured the waist of every party comer, People were paying 18, 19 and 20 cents to get in, We probably didn't measure any waist that were rounder in circumference than a 29.

Like all of our parties we supplemented by selling "Ripple" which was sold for 50 cents a bottle and every bottle was sold. In fact at this party and all of the others we almost never had enough but we would get it. See back then the “liquor store” closed at 10 o’clock and as you could imagine the party is just starting to get started at ten and the Ripple would be running low by 9 o’clock.

We would send somebody to make a mad dash to the store before it closed. We were buying Ripple by the case. We even cut a deal with the owner of the store, Skippy Jake, to buy at cut rate prices and to have a middle man pick up spot in case it was past 10. This shit was ingenious, remember, cell phones were unheard of, we are teenage boys pulling this kind of shit off with house phones and nothing else in between and was getting it done! Even the kids we called “conservative” back then and even white kids came to our parties. And we made absolutely certain that nothing happened to them either.

Freddie Little (STN)

In Loving Memory of Charles E. Franklin

1950 — 1995

SERVICES:

Saturday, August 26, 1995
10:00 A.M.

Campbell Funeral Chapel
1225 Calhoun Street, Trenton, New Jersey

Rev. Willie Granville

One of the Boys who I'd known and loved for a lifetime was Charles Edward " Eddie" Franklin. Eddie and I had known each other since we were five years old and his family like Muscle Head's family accepted me as one of their own. Eddie lived a street over from me, Wilson Street, around the corner, a backyard away. And while Eddie didn't box for the P.A.L., he was one of the best and the most willing street fighter I'd known. Even as a kid he would fight grown men and it never took a lot for him to get into it and he would do so at the drop of a hat, sometimes, it would happen so fast it was scary. And if you happened to be with Eddie, Lee Grant, Big Doug, Squeak Duncan and Butch "Monster" Page on a given night, it could get out of control to put it lightly.

With Love
Forever
LeRoy 5TH

BATTLE, DOUGLAS
118 Burton Ave.

I remember at the Waist party a couple of black guys roaring about white kids were in the party. We calmed that shit down almost immediately and gave forewarning that nothing, absolutely nothing should happen to any of the people who came to our party, black, white, conservative, nerd, it didn't matter, if you tried to hurt anybody who came to our parties there would be a serious price to pay. Mind you, we weren't gangsters, bullies, or tough guys nor did we purport ourselves, being as such. But what we were was a formidable group of boys who had formed an alliance, first with each other, and then with our friends and at the end of the day, while we didn't start fights with anyone or group, we made sure that we ended them with us on top! And what made us as formidable as we were is that, as aforementioned, we were boys from every part of the town and among teenagers who attended Trenton High; while we may not have been liked by everybody – there were "haters" back in the day too, we were known if not by everybody, we were known about by everybody!

(left to right) Kenny aka "Country," Picket aka Melvin Douglas, LeeRoy aka "BabyRoy," and Lindsey aka "Butch"/"Monster" @ Lee Grant's wedding reception.

We were there when Lee Grant was married, we were there when Eddie married Lee Grant's sister, we were there when Doc married Tanny and we were there when John Paul married Harriet.

Even some the older "Princes" and "Queens" loved us and knew who we were. Some of them even graced us with their presence at one and probably biggest party which was

"Tank"

A Home Going
Service
for

William
Stanley Lomon

A loving father and caring friend.

We have all lost a kind and generous man that has touched our lives. He will be truly missed. But his memory shall forever live on in our hearts. -The Family

Sunrise	Sunset
October 23, 1933	October 22, 2009

Services:
Thursday, October 29, 2009 at 11:00 A.M.

New Salem Baptist Church
116 Union Street
Trenton, New Jersey

Officiant:
Pastor Ernest Wormley

held at the old Pittsburgh Glass Company. We even hired Donald "The Fox" Carter

(left to right) LeeRoy aka “BabyRoy,” Donald aka “The Fox,” and “Boobey”

to come in and dance at the party. Our promotional gimmick was written on index cards; the invitation brand of the day, was "Come See Sister Mamie." For nearly a month kids would come up to us in school and ask who was Sister Mamie? We'd respond by telling them that if you wanted to find out, you'd have to come to the party. Shit, even most of us didn't know who Sister Mamie was and none of us had ever met her. See a few of us were introduced to Sister Mamie through a cut on a jazz recorded album composed by Yusef Lateef. Two of the cuts on this album were Sister Mamie and "Number 7" and we were introduced to both of them by Furman Counts, our jazz listening master. The few of us who had been introduced to Sister Mamie was because we were in regular attendance at the "Wednesday Night Affair" at Furman's crib.

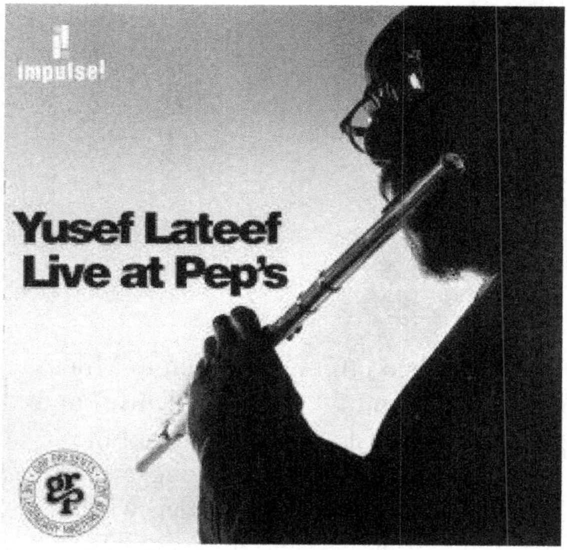

The "Wednesday Night Affair" was a night that was attended by any number of the members of the club, (no girls). It was a night that Furman's mom, would be working all night at the hospital. So in essence it was our night to have the house. The first order of the day was at least one $5 bag of "reefer." Ramadhan, aka "Bum Brown" as he was called back then, and was the was usually the person to go cop and the chief joint roller. He, Furman, Bubby, Rome and Doug were our reefer experts but Ramadhan was usually the one who copped the reefer and the one who rolled the joints. While the "smoke" may have been the primary component of the entre, it also included vodka, Miller Highlight and/or Colt 45 beer, Ripple and/or Bali Hai. Remember, this was back in the day, McDonald's wasn't happening, Gino's was Giant back then. So we'd have Gino's Giant burgers and buckets of Kentucky Fried Chicken and we'd eat, drink and smoke the night away.

The latter is putting it lightly, we'd get "fucked up." We'd listen to Miles Davis, John Coltrane, Sarah Vaughn's rendition of "Mack The Knife" and Yusef Lateef's "Number 7;" our favorite, and Sister Mamie. One of the legendary cats of our time was a dude by the name of Dan Livingston. Dan would periodically grace us with his presence. He was older, wiser, and more experienced about life, about reefer and about the world. Dan was legendary because he could fight. He was a tall, rangy, wiry, built guy, a middleweight who could not only box but he could punch. Dan used to come and smoke with us and we'd were excited to hear the *"tales of the crip," by Dan Livingston.* Dan, while he was a Trentonian, he was also a country boy and he spoke like he was but he was a joy to listened to and just to be in his presence was an honor for young boys like us.

Lee Grant Moses

Chapter 6: At The Hands Of My Brother/Home Grown Homicide

Gary Livingston, Willie “Blue Chip” Davis, Bobby Turner, Butch Clark, John Echoes, John Paul Lacey, Frank Johnson, James “Handsome” Ransom, Larry Bostik, Richard Nixon, Furman Counts, Anthony Williams, Joshua “Josh-Mo” Moore, Hightstown and Floyd Nolan were all Boys of My Summers. I knew each of them personally and they all died as a result of homicide/murder. Each of them died at the hands of someone who looked like them, walked like them and who talked like them. While the numbers are not huge they are very significant for Trenton, New Jersey and nearly all of them occurred before the proliferation of guns in the African American community, as nearly all of them have been dead for nearly; a combined, two generations. Most of them were killed in the 1960's; ('65, '66) and 1970's and all of them died; if compared to today, on the not so mean streets of Trenton, New Jersey.

Much later on, in the year 2000, another boy of my summers would join the ranks of those murdered in the streets of Trenton. He was born on August 20, 1968 when I was seventeen years old. We lived in the same home and were raised for a time by the same mother and grandmother. His name was Lamar Roy Brown-Jordan and he was my son. He was murdered on May 17, 2000, shot to death on the boulevard – Martin Luther King Boulevard, formerly Princeton Avenue. I was a teenage father, a junior in high school when he was born, who had fathered a premature little boy who just prior to his thirty second birthday would die a premature death as a result of a fatal gunshot injury.

Lamar or "Power" as he was known in the streets of Trenton and "Chuckie" to his family; although seventeen years younger and my son he was also one of the Boys of My Summers. He grew up with me too and he called my mother (Bernice) "Ma." He would come to know many of my friends and they would come to know him. He was one of us. Most of the murders of the boys unlike that of Lamar was not in the era of gangs. Trenton was not being overrun by "Bloods." Guns were nowhere near as accessible or plentiful and the greatest difference was that when we were growing up and someone was killed no homicides went unsolved. Eighteen years later Lamar's assailants have yet to be to be apprehended and brought to justice. The people who murdered him may still be free or are in prison convicted of other cases which may include homicide. We grew up in a different time and era and the police in Trenton had a different method of operation and they knew the people.

The corner ("The Strip) was also a different place. Without trying to glorify any of things that happened on the strip and there was much that happened (i.e., gambling, numbers, craps/dice, cards/skin game, drug dealing, drug using, pimps, whores, dikes, daffodils, preachers, politicians and police, as has been aforementioned herein, there was a different culture when it came to murder. See in those days it was clearly understood by both the hustlers on the corner and the police that the Five Points and The Strip was a business

miskeen

district, a place of illicit commerce and enterprise and that business must be conducted. This was an unwritten agreement between the police and the hustling community. It wasn't a secret, everybody knew it! Anytime a homicide occurred on the Five Points it meant that business would be seriously impacted and everyone understood it, the hustlers understood it and so did the police, namely and mainly the Hall brothers, both Homicide Detectives who drank at the Monument Lounge with the rest of us. As aforementioned, Trenton was a very different place when we were growing up. The police, especially those who were African American new us and we knew them. Some of them were our fathers, uncles, cousins, brothers, coaches, boy scout troop leaders; Mr. Holmes, drill team leaders; Mr. Bingham and next door neighbors. "Smitty" and the Sapps and the Hall brothers (two brother homicide detectives) and even some guys who grew up with us eventually joined the Trenton Police Department, among them, Wesley Richardson. Howard White, JohnnySapp. So when a homicide occurred we understood that not only did it mean trouble for the person who committed the act but we also knew that there would be consequences for everyone on every corner in the city until that person was apprehended. Simply put things heated up and people would tell you quickly that it's "Hot out here."

While no one openly “snitched;” at least not yet, there was a culture that existed that included conversations that made it clear that if anyone knew of the assailants whereabouts let him know he should turn himself in. Also most of us knew both the victim and the victimizer and most of the time both were our friends and anyone who was harboring the assailant was also a friend. There were no good guys or bad guys in this. The guy who got killed we knew and loved and the guy who killed him we knew and loved.

Our corner (The Strip) of the Five Points also had mediators, mentors, elders, respected hustlers, and counselors like Albert “Bo” Robinson sometimes, Freddie Glover, Happy Carmichael and when he was sane a cat we called “Big 12,” aka Jackie Ellis, and even the police themselves. But even with the unwritten cooperation agreement the police of our day were just different as well. There other cats like Charles “Dino” Holman who garnered a great deal of respect, while his demeanor was subtle he was a respected leader, one you always knew was present and his voice carried a lot of weight. Kenneth “Mule Train” Bethea was another voice on our corner who had say so that could straighten things out and so could Asim aka Regis Gates.

A Freddie Glover Signature

There was always a “Straight-ing” to be had in the Crap game held in the back of the Shalamar Barbershop and that task was left to Archie, the “Houseman” but there were others like Big Doug Posey, Puddin Housley and Bo Robinson! Yea Bo gambled with us, he made sure that periodically he dropped into the crap game and he wasn’t “eyeballing and attempting to bet;” as saying that was called out to cats who were just standing around and not gambling, he gambled and he didn’t bet scared, he’d bet to win and he was a right better and stood in front of the table and shot the dice, grunted and hollered like the rest of us trying to make the dice turn over to make the number. Bo was one of us, he lived and was raising his family on the 5 Points, he lived on Brunswick Avenue, he was a friend, a confidant, a peacemaker, a mediator, a counselor, a politician even when he didn’t hold a political office. There was a time he even gave almost all of the hustlers and players on the Strip a job at UPI and they in turn gave the rest of jobs.

Bo would even be called on by the Trenton Police Department. In one such case during the time when he still lived on Brunswick Avenue, he was called on to end a dispute and to affect an arrest of Jackie Ellis, aka "Big 12" who was in a face to face dispute with a well known dangerous Police Officer named Drew Smith.What caused the immediate incident, I was not clear, however what I was clear about was Drew Smith's reputation in our community and that reputation included a racist brutality the ended the lives of two members of the Trenton community. I also was clear about Big 12's brutality as he had demonstrated on more than one occasion including the brutal beatings of Happy Carmichael, Richard Nixon and the unwarranted assault on Earl Purnell and a number of others. 12 and Drew Smith were both big dudes, 6'5"-6'6', were face to face in front of the Hustlers Pool room, 12 was telling Drew Smith that he'd kill him, his mother, his father, his kids and dared him to attempt to arrest him, moments later police cars began arriving in droves and 12 continued to stand his ground. Someone, and I think it might have been one of the police officers, ask for Bo Robinson and minutes later Bo was there to mediate and to help de escalate the situation. What Bo actually facilitated was 12's arrest; amazing, and rode in the police car with him to the station. The katter illustrates the man's influence, how important he was to our community and what he meant to Trenton, and the kind of commitment and courage he had. Even his commitment to help some of the worst of us and 12 was one of the worst of us, may the creator be pleased with him.

Junior Mason: An Icon, Legend, Leader, Shot Caller and Entrepreneur

They were much more dedicated to solving murders. I honestly can't remember of any homicide that occurred; to my knowledge, that went unsolved. Moreover, I don't know of any, where it took more than three months, and that is a stretch, to apprehend the persons who committed the murder. Most of the time the person was apprehended in less than two weeks and most of them within days, just on police work alone. So homicides were unacceptable and as such murders occurred much less frequently than they do today because when there was a problem things were talked out, disputes including money disputes, wherever possible, were settled by the community. I can remember countless times when the question was asked, "Can You Stand a Straightening?" The latter was asking two or more people involved in the dispute whether the parties would allow an intervention from someone who may have knowledge or was an eye witness if you will, someone who's word could be taken and who was respected. Sometimes this would involve bets revolving around a number that showed up at the roll of the dice in a game of dice aka a crap game.

Bake and Melvin Douglas hugging, Ervin & Richard

These bets some time could involve hundreds and sometimes thousands of dollars and tensions could seriously rise about this kind of money. Sometimes it would involve someone who owed a debt and had not paid it and the debtor was not happy to the extent that he may seek retribution. When this was known to the community and it usually was, oftentimes someone would intervene including paying off the debt to the debtor and a payment plan would be made to retrieve what was owed by the debtor at a later date. The point here was to prevent business from being interrupted by violence that could include murder. However, if the truth be told, there were times that the violence that would and did occur could not be stopped. One such time is when "Goldie" (Melvin) badly beat up Booty Bronson. As violent as it was, it was also sad; at least in my eyes, because there was a time that Booty was on top and while not revered by everyone, he was one of the top money getters, not only on our beloved Strip but in our town. To have both witnessed the beating and Booty's fall from grace including his being all but shunned by our Godfather, Freddie Talerico, who at one time he served as a trusted confidant and money handler. The latter relationship would dramatically shift as the community would witness the signs of Booty's dope/coke addiction. And while Melvin beat Booty up about a number he called in the dice game, which was a bet involving Freddie and Melvin's money, I am convinced that it was also about Booty's decline in the eyes of almost everybody and Melvin's; like most of us, total loss of respect for him.

Not only did we have "Bo" Robinson but we also had Sammy Pack, while Bo was the undisputed, unelected Mayor of Trenton, Sammy Pack was a policy man who was one of the comptrollers of the numbers game on the Five Points. He worked for another black guy named "Pedro" who was said to be; at the time, the only black number banker in the State of New Jersey. This meant dealing with a lot of money, I mean a lot of money and Sammy Pack became one of the richest black men on the Strip. But he was a sweet dude, he handled his business always like a gentleman and he was respected by everyone. No matter who you were you could go to Sammy Pack and get a dollar or two, sometimes hundreds of dollars. This included people who he knew used drugs but if you didn't keep your word he wouldn't give you another dime if you failed to pay him back. He would never curse, holler, scream at anybody or threaten. He just didn't give you any more money. One of the other Godfathers of our Strip was Rambough. He wasn't on the Strip everyday however when he was you knew it. His demeanor was subtle yet it could be more pronounced especially if he saw you doing or getting ready to do the wrong thing he would let you know it. There were a couple of times that I was getting ready to step in to something; in this case, where something was already happening. He snatched me away from the entrance of the Monument Lounge. The place was filled with cops and everybody in the bar were getting ready to go to jail, everybody including number writers; policy men, shylarks aka loan sharks, bartenders and drug dealers with everybody being charged with drug possession because it was the second time in less than a month that drugs were tossed on the floor and nobody would take the weight. Well this time anybody who was inside took the weight as everybody got a bag of boy and a bag of girl, a "one and one!"

I remember when they came back to the corner and Picket (Austin); a number writer, was furious!! He didn't sell drugs, use drugs, like drugs or the people who sold or used them is how he put it. Hightstown, the neighborhood loan shark, was also pissed off. They had a meeting in the Shalammar Barbershop and it was that day that the rules changed. The rule from that day forward was if you threw something on the floor, you take the weight, simple as that and if you didn't, well!

But Rambough helped me not to get caught up in it and there would be more than once that he would pull my coat and make sure that I wasn't in the way. See, Rambough was a seasoned cat and we were young boys and wild as ape shit and he knew it. Yet he was gentle with us and on top if that we all knew he didn't take no shit and that he loved us and one of US was his son, Blair!

Rambough

But murder is murder and a homicide is a homicide no matter what era it happens in. In fact if the truth be told and this book is about telling the truth, the murder rate in the 1960's and '70's were some of the highest recorded in America since homicide statistics have been kept. There are periods in American history, the roaring twenties, the great depression, the civil rights era of the late 1960's and the height of the heroin trade of the 1970's that the murder rate in the nation have shown increases.

Yet era or no era the homicide rates among African American boys and men is atrocious. For decades now we have been killing one another with impunity. And nearly every one of us who is murdered is killed by someone who, looks like us, who walks like us and who talks like us. Some of us who were murdered were boys of my summers. Others of us who were murdered have been sons of the boys and girls that I grew up with. It is a pathological autoimmune homicidal suicide syndrome, a disease that has infected our children and spills blood on the very fabric of the city in which I was born. It was not all that long ago standing outside of the Wayne Avenue Baptist Church talking with Jesse Harris regarding the murders of his son and mine. It was painful for both of us, because it was painful when it happened, still painful now and will be painful forever.

COMMON TRAITS OF HOMICIDE VICTIMS & VICTIMIZERS

Victims and their victimizers are both likely:

- To be **young** and **male.**
- To be of the same race.
- To be poor
- To see themselves as being attacked, threatened or needing protection.
- May use or abuse alcohol, cocaine, PCP, or other drugs.
- May be depressed
- May be affected by present and/or post traumatic stress.
- Have had previous exposure to violence (seen violence inflicted, often on their mother or siblings or have been the victim of violence personally.

Source: Deadly Consequences: Prothrowstith/Weissmann 1991

Why did it happen then and why is happening now are questions I only seek to provide some semblance of an answer to, however, I am certain that I am somewhere in the ballpark while attempting to do so. African Americans, no matter what city we live in tend to always be outraged when a black boy, man or woman is killed by the police and we should always be outraged but we should be just as outraged by the fact that in ninety-eight percent of the cases when a black boy, man or woman is murdered in this country he or she is murdered by someone of his own race and almost always when the victim is male he is murder by someone who looks like him, wh like him and who talks like him.

I was working at "The Counseling and Treating People of Color Conference: An International Perspective" in San Juan, Puerto Rico in 1999. I had arrived at the conference in PR to present as a member of a panel. However, shortly after checking in I was informed that there were members of the panel who would not be attending the conference and I was told that I would have a lot more time to present and the lady who informed me said that she hoped that I was prepared. I was more than prepared, this was a dream come true. I work from the place that says "it is better to be prepared and not have an opportunity than to have an opportunity and not be prepared." My presentation was *"PHAATT"* (Peace, Hope, Ascension, Abundance, Tradition and Tranquility). As a component of the presentation I introduced the full conference to the "Autoimmune Homicidal Suicide Syndrome." As such I had no idea that the very next year; 2000, I would be presenting again at the Black Alcohol and Addiction Institute's conference in Atlanta, Georgia. Only this time my workshop would also include the details of the murder of my own son who was murdered in Trenton on May 17, 2000.

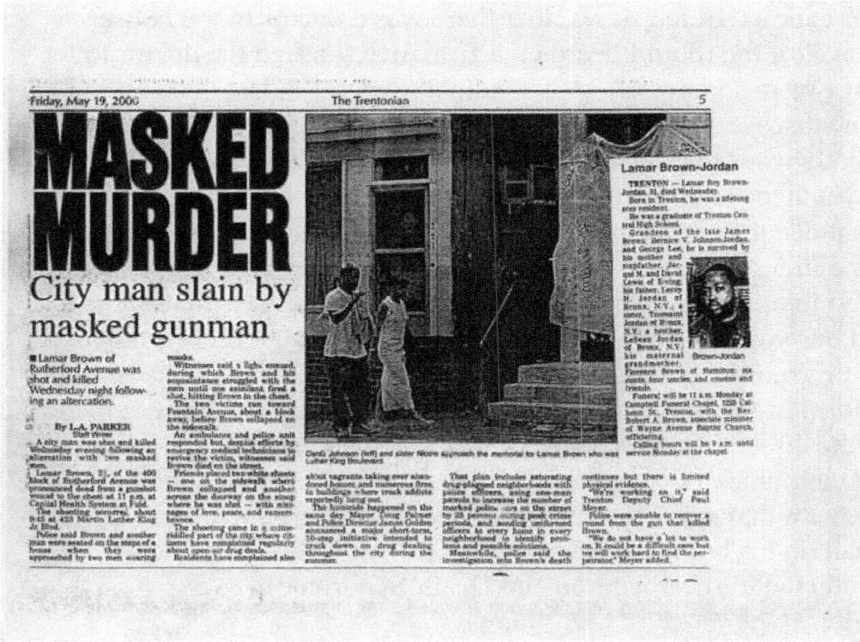

Friday, May 19, 2006 The Trentonian 5

MASKED MURDER

City man slain by masked gunman

■ Lamar Brown of Rutherford Avenue was shot and killed Wednesday night following an altercation.

By L.A. PARKER
Staff Writer

A city man was shot and killed Wednesday evening following an altercation with two masked men.

Lamar Brown, 31, of the 400 block of Rutherford Avenue was pronounced dead from a gunshot wound to the chest at 11 p.m. at Capital Health System at Fuld.

The shooting occurred about 9:45 at 423 Martin Luther King Jr. Blvd.

Police said Brown and another man were seated on the steps of a house when they were approached by two men wearing masks.

Witnesses said a fight ensued, during which Brown and his acquaintance struggled with the men until one assailant fired a shot, hitting Brown in the chest.

The two victims ran toward Fountain Avenue, about a block away, before Brown collapsed on the sidewalk.

An ambulance and police unit responded but, despite efforts by emergency medical technicians to revive the victim, witnesses said Brown died on the street.

Friends placed two white sheets — one on the sidewalk where Brown collapsed and another across the doorway on the stoop where he was shot — with messages of love, peace, and remembrance.

The shooting came in a crime-riddled part of the city where citizens have complained regularly about open-air drug deals.

Residents have complained also about vagrants taking over abandoned houses and numerous fires in buildings where crack addicts reportedly hang out.

The homicide happened on the same day Mayor Doug Palmer and Police Director James Golden announced a major short-term, 10-step initiative intended to crack down on drug dealing throughout the city during the summer.

That plan includes saturating drug-plagued neighborhoods with police officers, using one-man patrols to increase the number of marked police cars on the street by 25 percent during peak crime periods, and sending uniformed officers to every home in every neighborhood to identify problems and possible solutions.

Meanwhile, police said the investigation into Brown's death continues but there is limited physical evidence.

"We're working on it," said Trenton Deputy Chief Paul Meyer.

Police were unable to recover a round from the gun that killed Brown.

"We do not have a lot to work on. It could be a difficult case but we will work hard to find the perpetrator," Meyer added.

Dardi Johnson (left) and sister Nicole approach the memorial to Lamar Brown who was [illegible] Luther King Boulevard.

Lamar Brown-Jordan

TRENTON — Lamar Roy Brown-Jordan, 31, died Wednesday.

Born in Trenton, he was a lifelong area resident.

He was a graduate of Trenton Central High School.

Grandson of the late James Brown, Bernice V. Johnson-Jordan, and George Lee, he is survived by his mother and stepfather, Jacqui M. and David Lewis of Ewing; his father, Leroy H. Jordan of Bronx, N.Y.; a sister, Tanmaini Jordan of Bronx, N.Y.; a brother, LeSean Jordan of Bronx, N.Y.; his maternal grandmother, Florence Brown of Hamilton; six aunts, four uncles and cousins and friends.

Brown-Jordan

Funeral will be 11 a.m. Monday at Campbell Funeral Chapel, 1220 Calhoun St., Trenton, with the Rev. Robert A. Brown, associate minister of Wayne Avenue Baptist Church, officiating.

Calling hours will be 9 a.m. until service Monday at the chapel.

507 Martin Luther King Boulevard, Trenton, New Jersey

I remember calling out to ask whether there was a doctor in the house. From the back of the room I heard an affirmative. I asked the doctor to let me know if I were somewhere in the ballpark when I'd described an autoimmune disease such as rheumatoid arthritis – "simply put, I said, it's when the body loses tolerance for itself." The doc confirmed for the conference audience that I was indeed in the ballpark. Homicides, murders that occur in the African American community are an autoimmune illness. We have turned on ourselves because we have lost the ability to internalize the meaning and spirit of who we actual are as a people and our young people who are those who are the largest group of victims of this morbid pathological killer are affected by the most profound form of this immune deficiency. We have lost the ability to recognize the "free radicals" that are attacking our spirits. The latter is because the immune deficiency of the illness has erased any notion of the African proverb that says, "I am because we are, we are therefore I am." Joe Marshall, in his book "Street Soldiers" calls it "Hood Disease," = "AIDS (Addicted to Incarceration and Death Syndrome)."

Lamar Roy “Chuckie/Power” Brown-Jordan

“Where I’m From, the social atmosphere is dense with animosity and dread. There looms a collective feeling of despair so palatable that it seems to be contagious.”

Sanyika Shakur: Monster

Homicide begins as a mortality factor in the first year of life for black boys in America. Murder is the second leading cause of death, after "accidents (unintentional injuries)" for African American boys beginning at age one. It is the second (2nd) leading cause of death after accidents (unintentional injuries) between ages 1-4 and it is the fourth (4th) leading cause of death for black boys 5-9 and moves back to the second (2nd) leading cause of death for those 10-14 and then catapults to the leading cause of death for black boys and men ages 15-19, 20-24 and 25-34 and the third (3rd)leading cause of death after "unintentional injuries" for black men ages 35-44 and is the seventh leading cause of death for those of us 45-54. Black boys and men are at risk of homicide for nearly 80% of our lives as it doesn't stops being a leading cause of death for us; as a group, until we are age 54. However, the latter does not mean that we don't get killed at age 54 and beyond, what it means is that it (homicide) stops being a leading cause of death and its correlation to our life expectancy; age 70, as a group.

One of the most illuminating examples of homicide extending beyond age 54 can be found inside of the annals of crime springing from Trenton, New Jersey in the murder of 84-year-old; The Honorable, Mr, Jerry Eure, Sr., a Tuskegee Airman and World War II Veteran and Hero, who was brutally murdered in his home on Edgecombe Avenue located in the West Ward of Trenton. And like most homicides in the African American diaspora Mr. Eure was murdered by someone who was known to him. Mr. Eure was killed by a young neighbor, Anthony Bethea.

{Photo) Anthony Bethea N.J. Department of Corrections

Honorable Jerry Eure, Sr.

As is the case in nearly every case of black male homicides, nearly every one of those who died as a result of having been murdered in Trenton was killed by someone that they knew. While I will only mention the names of assailants who are no longer living and victims they killed. I will make reference to other cases in which the assailant is still living and want both to protect their privacy and their names, as they are also boys of my summers who were and still to this day are my friends. John Echoes was killed by Earl Taylor and Butch Clark and Bobby Turner were killed by Toby Scrivens all of who help to make up the list of the more than two hundred of those on the list of the dead who once were alive and lived and grew up in Trenton, New Jersey. Echoes was killed when Earl shot him to death over, reportedly, a two dollar bet in a dice game outside of Paulie's Corner, Monmouth Street in the Wilbur Section of Trenton.

Toby Scriven killed both Butch Clark and Bobby Turner on the same night that they'd robbed him of a parcel of dope (heroin) in South Trenton. They were killed in a house on Asbury Street. Butch Clark died that night and Bobby Turner, after hanging on to life for about two weeks, finally succumbed to his injuries. Toby killed Butch and Bobby with the double blast of a double barreled shotgun. This, as anyone could imagine was a vicious murder exacted because Toby was wronged and took out life ending, deadly revenge. Toby's revenge as homicides can sometimes be was swift and almost immediate. And as was the case in these two murders, everyone involved the victim, the victimizer and their families knew one another. And when I say knew one another, I'm talking about guys who saw each other every day, who hung out with each other, went to the same schools, played together, lived on the same street or in the same neighborhood community, Butch, Bobby and Toby were South Trenton boys.

All too often these murders are referred to as senseless, especially in black context. However, actually they or at least many of them are more complex. In fact if we would only venture to connect the dots, they make perfect sense. They are oftentimes carried out by someone who believes like Toby that he has been violated, bullied, disrespected, taken advantage of and whatever the original causal factor may have been the former victim, as in Toby's case, begins to operate out of an age old component of intentional interpersonal injury called the "Principle."

"The Principle" can be a toxic ingredient; like trauma, that fuels the process of homicides beyond the instant transgression and embodies itself inside a self-righteous indignation that shapes itself into pure, extreme and deadly rage. The fact that Butch and Bobby believed that they could rob Toby; and did so, also meant that they also believed that he was insignificant enough to carry out their dastardly act but what they'd not paid attention to was "The Principle" and how it can, does and will continue to manifest and transform itself into an autoimmune response that can be best explained outside of the traditional books of psychology and psychiatry but has a nexus to these through the development of a diagnostic impression and a prognosis that can be found in the archives of the genre of "Hip-Hop" on the tracks of an album by Jay-Z entitled "Reasonable Doubt:"

"We Invite You To Something Epic
Where We Hustle Out Of A Sense Of Hopelessness
A Sorta Desperation
And Through That Desperation
We Become Addicted
Like The fiends that We Are Accustomed To Serving
Where We Feel We Have Nothing To Lose
Where We Offer You, Well, We Offer Our Lives
What Do You Bring To The Table?"

In my opinion we suffer from a form of an Autoimmune Disease that has infected us and is a disorder that ought to be chronicled in the "Diagnostic Statistical Manual of whatever number as a psychological and psychiatric disorder as defined herein:

"The Autoimmune Homicidal Suicide Syndrome is a violent hypersensitive reaction caused by the inability to recognize the relational-kinship to one's brethren; to clearly distinguish between one's self and the destructive pathological and foreign entities which produce a lethal reaction against one's kind/self, while failing to recognize and respond to actual threats within and outside of self/kind, which thereafter results in homicide and the destructive eradication of one's own interest, prospects and continued existence or suicide"
LeeRoy Jordan

Cliffy Armstrong was killed by his younger brother, John Paul Lacey was killed by a friend who will go nameless herein, Larry Bostick was killed by a friend who's name will not be mentioned, Furman Counts was killed in Wilbur Section by assailants unknown to the writer, Gary was killed by a close friend who will not be identified herein. Jackie Robinson killed Robert "Rat" Antley both of who are on the list of the dead. Floyd Nolan was also murdered by someone he knew and who was known by everybody else who knew the both of them.

Most of the deaths of the boys on the list can be attributed to homicide, drug overdose/ drug suicides, HIV and suicide. None of them can be attributed to what is referred to as "natural causes" or "old age."

On an October night in 1971 James "Handsome" Ransom was shot and killed on the Strip. Many of my friends and I were celebrating our birthdays at Delores Ann's house on Ingram Avenue. It was Annie's birthday but Dot and I also were born in the same month only a few days apart. It was at the party around 11:00 p.m. that the word came in that Ransom had been shot and was believed to have been pronounced dead at the scene. Ransom as most of us called him was a very good looking dude, who in my opinion had a lot of class and style. As it turned out Ransom's murder was a contract hit carried out by a young kid out of Cincinnati, Ohio. The kid, who I did not know, although I was in the Mercer County Jail at the same time as he was, in 1971, as the case unfolded was contracted for the hit by a dude out of New York City named "Dickie Diamond."

Ransom and several other high profile dudes from the Strip were reported to have had been involved in the dope game; heroin, with this cat Dickie Diamond. The story was that Ransom and several others had taken packages of dope from this dude and had failed to produce the money for the product. Back in the day the drug trade was about giving out "work," meaning dope or coke or whatever the drug, on consignment. A price was given for the package and you took the work on your word. It seemed that none of the Trenton guys had kept their word and Ransom became a casualty of the trade and others were said to be running scared. These were big name dudes as far as Trenton was concerned, one of who was a cat named Booty Bronson. At one time he was one of the richest dudes on the Strip and carried clout, he had status. When the numbers came out, if it was 845 or 516 everyone on the Strip new that Booty had hit for tens of thousands, 40, 50, 60 grand kind of hits. But the word was that he and one of my heroes; Earl Purnell, and mentor were also the subject of contract hits.

Fortunately, several weeks later the kid out of Ohio was caught and shortly thereafter so was Dickie Diamond. As I said earlier in those days murders were solved quickly or at least those who murdered were apprehended quickly. In 1972 Dickie Diamond was sentenced to 30 years in state prison. I was an inmate in the Mercer County Workhouse in March of '72 when he was being transported to Trenton State Prison. I remember saying to him as he passed that he could leave the bad leather coat he was wearing with me because he wouldn't be needing it, where he was going. Beside that Ransom was one of my favorite guys. He was a true player and a nice cat, stylish and fly, one of the first dudes to perm his hair; "Superfly." and he was the real deal.

The Strip was in mourning for several days and there was also an eerie kind of tension and fear hanging in the air, a kind of collective paranoia. Ransom was a star and he'd been killed on our precious Strip and murder was something that happened but the times that it did were few and far between. So to have one of ours murdered and especially by some out of town dudes shook up our corner leaving us in a condition of shock and traumatic stress.

There would be another murder at the Five Points a little more than a year later. While this murder would involve black men the difference would be the victim was a white man. But he was no ordinary white man he was Jimmy Talarico a Five Point Icon and co-owner of Freddie's Famous Steak House. Jimmy and Freddie were brothers, Italian guys who we loved. On a cold December night after closing, Jimmy and employees of the steak house had crossed North Warren Street into the park on their way home. It was believed that Jimmy was carrying the night's receipts. They were confronted by three black men who announced that it was a stick up. In the confrontation Jimmy was shot and later died. Again the Strip was in turmoil. While Jimmy didn't hang out with us like his brother Freddie, he was known to us just as well as Freddie and was a constant on the corner. Freddie's Famous Steak House was not just a steakhouse but an institution where any number of the people who frequented the strip also worked at the steak house. We were like family and to have a family member murdered was crazy. The Strip was changing and heroin addiction was at the center of that change and Jimmy Tal's murdered was an indirect consequence of the trade.

What seemed like only days after Jimmy's murder we would all be in for another shock as the police arrived on the corner as they often did. But this time they arrested a guy who I loved. At the time of his arrest the thinking of everyone in the know is that he was being arrested for selling drugs because at the time that is what he was doing and he was selling a winner, meaning that he was getting "paid!" That's why we were shocked beyond belief that he was actually arrested and being charged with the murder of Jimmy Tal. Not only was it beyond belief but it also didn't make any sense, any sense at all.

First, as I said, my man was getting paid. The dope he was selling was moving like wildfire. Besides that, he was known to Jimmy Tal like a father knows a son, or a next door neighbor knows the kid who grew up next door. There was just no way that a cat who was getting thousands everyday would rob and murder someone and let alone someone he was known by. Moreover, this guy was just not a robber, he was a thoroughbred hustler who would have never stooped so low.

In fact after he came home from a federal rehab stay in Lexington, Kentucky, he had a period when he was doing extremely bad. He wasn't the same Bill Thompson we'd all come to know, he was broke, wore the same denim outfit everyday for more than a month. He told me that all of his clothes had been stolen, sold or just disregarded by the woman he was with prior to going to Lexington.

It would seem to this writer that if he didn't rob or kill Jimmy or anyone else when he was doing extremely bad why would he wait until he was making money; and lots of it, every day and then decide to rob and kill a man who he knew and who knew him.

It just didn't make any sense. What we later learned is that there was another arrest in Jimmy's murder and it was the brother of my man who is one of the boys on the list. My man and his brother were both sentenced to life in prison. Ironically, his brother who was one of the assailants that night left prison on appeal.

He was never exonerated, his brother and left prison while Bill stayed down nearly fifteen years before being paroled. I remember talking to him some years after he was released and he told me that he'd been informed by parole officials that he did not have to report anymore. He said it was the besides being married to his wife Sissy, who by the way he married while in the earliest years of his prison sentence, and being let out of bondage, it was probably one of the best things that had ever happened to him.

Bill, I am convinced, guided by the forces of resilience and the ultimate grace of the deity that this writer believes created the universe and all things, even evolution, who provides breezes of redemption, which is the spirit of the creators genius and that which allowed Bill to survive a horrible injustice by his having survived and walked out of prison into the loving arms of his wife who rode this title wave with him from the first to last day continued to ride with him until his last breath.

"Mr. Bill"
In Loving Memory
of
William
Thompson
A loving husband and devoted father and caring friend
We have all lost a kind and generous Christian man that has touched our lives. He will be truly missed. But his memory shall forever live in our hearts -The Family
Funeral Services:
Kingdom Church
Interment

CHAPTER SEVEN: Trenton Makes The World Takes: Murder Capital of the Delaware Valley

Trenton has become a murder capital of the Delaware Valley, in which it sits and in fact it holds its own as one of the most dangerous small cities in America. At the end of 2013 Trenton had broken a record for an all-time high for murders in the city's history. Thirty-two, mostly young black men were murdered in Trenton in 2013, the deadliest year in the city's history. And those who weren't African American were Latino.

The Delaware Valley is comprised of four major cities, Trenton the Capital City of New Jersey, Camden; the region's poorest and one of New Jersey's largest cities, Philadelphia, Pa. and Wilmington, Delaware. In 2012, Camden broke its record of 58 murders surpassing its worst year for homicides since 1995, that at year's end, there were 65 people left dead as victims of this nationwide and regional pandemic in what used to be a town of superior commerce as was Trenton and the rest of the region in its hay day. Yet the truth be told homicides in Trenton, as I've already spoken to, is obviously not new to Trenton or anywhere else that they occur on a daily basis. What is different comparable to the era in which we grew up is that while people were murdered, they were the people who were supposed to be murdered. The latter represents the fact that the killings that happened in the 1960s and 1970s in Trenton were murders where no little children or other innocent bystanders were caught in the crossfire. There were no murders that this writer can recall where someone randomly shot into a crowd, at a block party or peace rally or community event. The second difference is that the Trenton Police Department, in particular the Hall brothers who were both homicide detectives solved nearly all homicides; especially those aforementioned, the perpetrator was apprehended within a matter of days and no longer than several weeks. It is my recollection that no homicides went unsolved.

The stark difference today is that too many homicides in Trenton, as in the case of communities of color throughout the country, homicides go unsolved and turn into 'cold cases' are all too frequent and have to the chagrin of the police department, parents, relatives; clergy and political leaders it has become the norm.

One such case is the one that is closest to the author. It is the case of Lamar Roy "Chuckie/Power" Brown-Jordan, who was murdered on May 17, 2000 near the corner of Fountain Avenue and Martin Luther King Boulevard formerly known as Princeton Avenue, literally a stone's throw away from where I first met his mother, who lived on Fountain Avenue. As of May 17, 2018 it has been eighteen years since he was gunned down on the Boulevard and no suspect or assailant has ever been arrested or prosecuted and the case has gone unresolved for nearly two decades.

This phenomena is one of epidemic proportion, a pandemic playing itself out throughout the Delaware Valley, including Philadelphia, Pennsylvania, Chester, Pennsylvania, Wilmington, Delaware, Camden and Trenton, New Jersey. In fact, as a region, the Delaware Valley could in fact be considered one of the most dangerous regions in the United States of America. Yet the pandemic is nationwide, from large metropolis like Chicago to smalls cities like Trenton and Chester, Pa., murder is everywhere.

When you examine the history and ask the question as to why we are murdering each other with impunity; like other places in the country where this pandemic of homicide, genocide, gendercide, fratricide (killing your own brother or sister) and suicide, exist, as far as Trenton is concerned; or anywhere else for the matter, it is this writer's belief that there is a profound and significant historical link, a connection, a nexus, a beginning, a correlation to the early demise of the "Boys of My Summers" and what is happening in Trenton today.

"AND IT DON'T STOP"

The Honorable, late John Henrik Clarke said, "that the events of 5000 years ago, will determine what happens 5 years from now, 50 years from now, 500 years from now, 5000 years from now, because all history is a current event."

Even after a "Civil Rights Movement" and a "Black Power Movement" and a "Pan Africanist Movement," the Trenton, Newark, Philadelphia, Detroit, Watts, and South Central Los Angeles riots in spite of Rosa Parks, Medgar Evers, the Honorable Elijah Muhammad, Malcolm X, Dr. Martin Luther King, Sojourner Truth, Harriet Tubman, H. Rap Brown, George Jackson, Angela Davis, Sonia Sanchez, Denmark Vesey, Nat Turner, Stokely Carmichael, John Lewis, Andrew Young, Jesse Jackson,

the "Underground Railroad," The March on Washington, the Voters Rights Act, The Million Man March, the election of the first African American President in U.S. History and thousands of other events and people who stand on top of the dry bones of our ancestors, and who fought for
freedom, justice and equality, in spite of these, we have still internalized the behavior of our former oppressors and those outside of our race who continue to oppress and kill us.

And it don't Stop!

Murder By Any Other Name: Both Ends of The Spectrum

Murder, called by any other name, is still murder. The Boys and I were alive when Medgar Evers was murdered, when President John Fitzgerald Kennedy was assassinated, when Malcolm X was murdered and when the Reverend Doctor Martin Luther King was assassinated and when Presidential Candidate; brother of slain President John F. Kennedy, Robert Kennedy was shot to death, we were all still alive. On November 22, 1963, I was a 13 year old, 7th grade student at Jr. High School #1. We were in English Class when our teacher, Mr. Aldube left and return to the class and exclaimed, "children, the President has just been shot!" Mr. Aldube was always dramatic. He taught english as if it were a Shakespearean play. He was tall and then with a huge adam's apple and his white shirt collars were always wrinkled, he looked like a character, Ichabod Crane, out of Washington Irving's story the "Legend of Sleepy Hollow." So we laughed because we thought he was acting again, however, we soon realized that he wasn't acting and he wasn't joking, we could see students lining up in the hallway and our class would join them, school was being dismissed.

When one researches and explores the archives of the Federal Bureau of Investigation (FBI) one will discover another word for murder "Legal

Intervention," The latter, simply put, is when people are "legally" killed by a law enforcement officer, i.e., the Police. Black Boys and Men lead the nation in the rate of death due to and caused by "Legal Intervention" (LI). Like other morbidity and mortality episodes and factors LI is an aggressive phenomenon that like so-called "Black on Black" murder, goes on unabated.

During the writing of this book I learned of other terms or even a paradigm; a model, for how and why police culture has, for years, so easily justify the murder of citizens, especially those who are black, male and unarmed. It is called "The Corruption of Noble Cause." The latter corruption finds its place cemented in the marrow of the bones of "police ethics." Noble Cause Corruption is guided by the age old belief that the ends always justify the means even when the means is both corrupt and illegal. It is corruption that is entered into with the expressed self-righteous belief and power that It will benefit the greater good. And this greater good is the desirable goal to "get rid of bad people" and there is no doubt in this writer's mind that a significant plurality of so called "bad people" are black like me.

In recent years we have watched the Corruption of the Noble Cause play itself out again and again in video after video of the killing of Black men by the police where almost no one is held accountable, leaving police corruption and misconduct to operate with impunity, "committed in the name of good ends" and the dismantling process and the immoral application of the death penalty before arrest, charges, trial, prosecution and a finding of guilty by a jury of one's peers. It, this corruption, hides itself in the supposed ethical conduct of individual police officers who are protected by the cloak of the "Blue Wall of Silence" that ensures that all police officers, even good ones, are trapped in a system where people are convinced that they can, will and have done and will do again, anything within their power, even illegally, to make the world safer. The latter has evolved into a pathological and universally warp, frightening and all too often lethal police police culture that was evidenced in the killing of Laquan McDonald, who was shot sixteen (16) time's by Chicago Police

Officer, Jason Van Dyke, who was convicted of Second Degree Murder and was sentenced to 6 years 9 months. Van Dyke's sentence itself is embroiled in the noble cause of corruption not only by the Police but also by the Courts in which they stand in judgement.

We are being murdered at ***"Both Ends of the Spectrum."*** The latter is a riveting "Lifeshop" developed by the writer and presented for the first time at the Beyond the Prison Walls Healthcare and Reentry Summit in Philadelphia, Pennsylvania. On one end of the spectrum; on a daily basis, we are killed at the hands of one another, on the other end, almost everyday in America we are killed by the police. It doesn't seem to matter if we are a so-called "Good Guy with a Gun" as was the case for both Emantic "EJ' Fitzgerald Bradford, Jr. or Jemel Roberson both of who were killed by police while attempting to save the lives of people in an Alabama mall, in the case of Emantic and in a Chicago nightclub in the case of Jemel. Both Jemel and Emantic were legally authorized to carry a firearm and in both cases each of them tried to save the lives of others from the acts of a "bad guy with a gun!" Black people in general and Black men in particular and especially, don't have the right to be a good guy with a gun nor do we have a 2nd Amendment right to keep and to bear arms while also not having the right of equal protections under the law. Or that you are 12 year old Tamir Rice playing with a toy gun and who was never given an iota of an opportunity to drop the gun, no warning, no siren, no nothing except to be immediately executed.

And even when we are at home in our own apartment, where we have keys and where we pay rent and lay our heads down, are unarmed and minding our business, the police can enter our home, shoot us to death and then claim that (she) thought she was in her apartment and that the young man she just murdered in his apartment was an intruder. Such was the case in the murder of Botham Shem Jean who was murdered by a police officer; Amber Guyger, on September 6, 2018 for no other reason than being home while being Black! Or we are choked to death, like Eric Garner, for allegedly selling loose cigarettes on a street corner in Staten

Island, New York. Eric Garner was choked to death while millions of us watched it happen in real time.

Or should you have been Jordan Davis or Trayvon Martin who were murdered because white men believed they had the absolute right to kill these young Black boys, just because, they were standing their ground.

(top) Ematic Bradford, Jr., Jewel Roberson (bottom)

Botham Shem Jean

George Jackson: “Blood In My Eye”

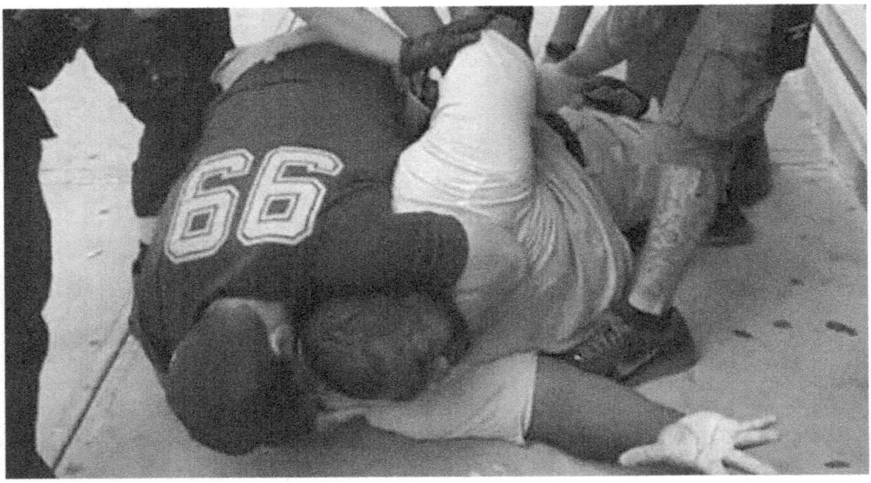

The Choke:

Jordan Edwards

Tamir Rice

Normandy High School
St. Louis County, Missouri

Michael Brown

Trayvon Martin

Therefore, we do not have to reinvent the wheel to stop this madness among our own people. And what we can do is to do everything we can to prevent our dying before our time. We can embrace ancient philosophies and mythologies inclusive of Sankofa, going back to retrieve that which we have left behind.

We ought to attach ourselves to the value and virtue of awareness; the premises springing from the spirit mind and voice of Lujan Matus; "**T***he most profound state of awareness comes from being devoted to your present circumstances, absorbing the sorrows and joys of others, so that you may see yourself within them, which is actually is you," and others.* We ought to tell the truth to and a about ourselves, taking a page from the writings of *Kiese Laymon; in "Heavy,"* who says he *wanted to write*

about "our families' relationship with simple carbohydrates, deep-fried meats, and high-fructose corn syrup." Yet listening to him on an NPR podcast he says his book is a long letter to his mother about *'the weight of lies; the weight of history" and*
"about language, and the words we use to hide violence or to inflict violence on others."

For those of us still here we can challenge ourselves, talk to ourselves, prepare ourselves and stand up for and to ourselves as a collective and embrace and participate inside of what I have entitled the "Ashe System;" Arthur Ashe: ***"Start where 'we' are, use what 'we' have and do what 'we' can!***

Message from the Elders

Keeping It Real For Real

by LeeRoy Jordan, Jr.

In the spirit of Each One Teach One, we introduce this new column in Harlem Overheard called "Message From The Elders." While Harlem Overheard is a youth-focused publication, we believe that the Elders in our community represent acres of diamonds in information and inspiration. In each edition of the paper a guest Elder will appear on this page to share seeds of inspiration, support and success for our young readers.

It's 7:22 Sunday morning, March 9, 1997. I've been informed by a young Black man whom I do not know that he has heard that Notorious B.I.G. (aka Biggie Smalls/Christopher Wallace) has been murdered in Los Angeles, California.

I am not shocked nor am I surprised by this news. Biggie Smalls has become another Black male victim of the "Hood Disease" A.I.D.S. (Addicted to Incarceration and Death Syndrome). "Hood Disease" or "A.I.D.S." is a contagious, genocidal, homicidal, suicidal pathology that is running rampant through communities of color with impunity and without respite. In 1994 we lost 10,083 Black male lives to homicide and "legal intervention."

For the past 15 years I have worked everyday of my life with hundreds of young men, of color in particular, all trapped in the clutches of a juvenile/criminal justice system that is feverishly working to return us to the antiquated moors of the 16th and 17th century.

The juvenile justice system is regressing to the Middle Ages when punishment for crimes were the same for children as they were for adults, inclusive of children being sentenced to death.

Listen up young people!!! The new proposals brought forth by the governor of New York state include:

* Tougher sentences for violent juveniles: Increasing the minimum sentence authorized for juvenile offenders by 50%.
* Fingerprinting any youth arrested for a felony offense.
* Forfeiture of Youthful Offender (YO) status upon a second felony conviction within five years and sentencing the youth as a repeat felon.
* Transferring responsibility for the custody of violent juvenile offenders over 16 from the Division For Youth (DFY) to adult prisons.

The above are just a few of the reforms that have been proposed and re-proposed by the governor of this state. Additionally, according to DFY, 30-month recidivism rates in 1989 and 1995 studies for Black, Latino, and White youth combined were 71%, 62%, and 49% for re-arrest, conviction, and incarceration respectively.

DFY does a fantastic job with our young people on the inside, thus we must do a better job with them on the outside. Listen up young people!!! Educate, educate, educate, and spread the word.

Young people need to know the real truth in the name of "Keeping it Real." When I travel to organizations throughout New York and other cities, I ask young people who commits most of the crime in America and the response is always the same, "Black people and Latinos."

This is the response because I believe that "power is the ability to define reality and to have others respond to that definition as their own." The truth is that Black and Latino people do not represent the majority of people arrested for crimes in America and never have.

It is the Elders who must do a much more thorough and complete job of dispelling this myth.

However, Black and Latino children represent over 90% of the juvenile admissions into DFY in New York State. Black and Latino males between 14-17 years of age represent the largest group of victims as a result of intentional interpersonal injury and in the case of Black males, including Tupac Shakur and Christopher (Biggie) Wallace, we have lost over 90,000 lives to homicide since 1986.

These casualties have nothing to do with Hip Hop and everything to do with violence. The same violence that took the life of Innis Cosby, Marvin Gaye, Sam Cooke, Lee Morgan, Donald Goines, George Jackson, Mark Clark, Fred Hampton, Malcolm X, Martin Luther King, Medgar Evers, and.... a violence that is preventable but gone unchecked by those of us who are most often its victims.

Young people have the potential to embrace PHAATT lives if they move toward and embrace PHAATT (Peace * Hope * Abundance * Ascension * Tradition * Tranquility) principles. These principles should be supported on a foundation built of MAAT: (Truth * Justice * Order * Harmony * Balance * Reciprocity *Righteousness/Prosperity) an ancient system of values and tradition bequeathed to your generation by our gracious ancestors. At the center, we should place the seven principles of the NGUZO SABA (Unity * Self-Determination * Collective Work and Responsibility * Cooperative Economics * Purpose * Creativity * Faith) and with this pyramid, a solid rock of tradition and value, we can live forever.

But we must be vigilant and we must take action. Move away from the "Thug Life" and "gangsterism" NOW!!! We are not a people of gangsters or thugs and there is no SAFE place on the earth for those who embrace thugism and gangsterism without the horrible consequences that we are witnessing today.

Until young people and Elders alike begin to take responsibility for who we are now and the great people that (we can become) must return to, the "Prison Industrial Complex" and DEATH will continue to consume our young.

It is both immoral and suicidal that young people can purchase a 22oz. bottle of potent malt liquor ($.99) for less than a 16oz. bottle of Snapple ($1.00). Complicity and SILENCE will lead to the total destruction of our community. We must stop living in peaceful co-existence with SIN, GIN, and JUICE.

We must stop being spectators in our own war. To continue to be spectators is to BE COLLABORATORS AND CONSPIRATORS IN OUR COLLECTIVE DEMISE.

And young people, know this. "He who prescribes the diameter of your thinking also controls the circumference of your activity." Keep it real and put the CODE of Life to the streets.

Code of Conduct
No drive by shootings against each other.
No random killings of each other.
No drug dealing in the hood and no dealing death among our people.
No collaboration with those that would destroy us.
NO FORTIES, NO GUNS, NO WEED........NO JAIL, NO DEATH.

Always remember tradition and that means HIP HOP stands on the shoulders of BE-BOP and there ain't no JAZZ without the BLUES, and this is the GOSPEL truth because HIP HOP is about "Keeping It Real."

Peace, Love, Respect
From an Elder

LeeRoy Jordan, Jr. is Founder and Chairman of African American Men United to Save Our Lives (A.A.M.U.S.O.) and the Clinical Coordinator of the LEGIT Youth Entrepreneurship Program of the Osborne Association, Inc.

Kenneth C. Chamberlin, Sr.

photo from eji report: "*Soldiers of infantry who won the Croix de Guere for gallantry in action 1919*

Nearly eight years ago, on November 19, 2011, Kenneth C. Chamberlin, age 68, a retired a 20 year veteran of the Westchester County, New

York's Department of Corrections and a retired veteran of the United States Marine Corps was shot to death by the police while in his home in White Plains, New York. Why was he killed and how? Mr. Chamberlain used a "LifeAid medical alert which by all accounts accidently went off that day which initiated a police response. Yet despite the fact that he told the police that he was okay and did not need help his door was kicked in, he was thereafter tasered and then shot to death. On the day he was murdered, Mr. Chamberlin joined a long line of black veterans who have served their country with honor and valor in every war, who have been murdered by the police after returning from battle in the fight for freedom throughout the world only to be killed by those whose freedoms they'd fought to preserve. In a report; "Lynching In America: Targeting Black Veterans, published by the Equal Justice Initiative (EJI) the plight and the history of black veterans is chronicled in its report: "Between the end of Reconstruction and the years following World II, thousands of black veterans were accosted, assaulted, attacked and many were lynched. Black veterans died at the hands of mobs and persons acting under the color of official authority; many survived near-lynchings; and countless others suffered severe assaults and social humiliation. Documenting these atrocities is vital to understanding the incongruity of our country's professed ideals of freedom and democracy while tolerating ongoing violence against people of color within our own borders. As a veteran and later a civil rights leader Hosea Williams said *"I had fought in World War II, and I once was captured by the German army, and I want to tell you the Germans never were as inhumane as the State Troopers of Alabama."*

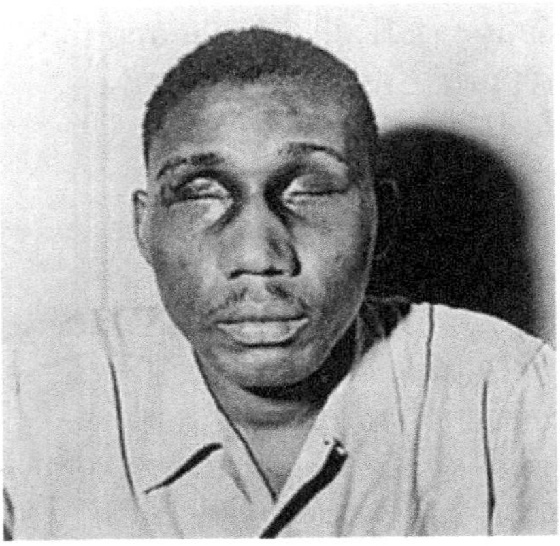

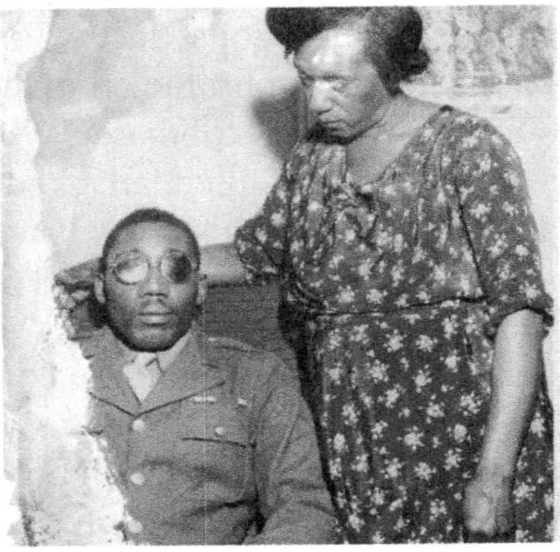

Isaac Woodard

Isaac Woodard, a World War II veteran of valor, having been decorated for his wartime service and having been honorably discharged, lived the rest of his life as a sightless person, not blinded by an injury occurring during his time in battle but rather his eyes were gouged out by a South Carolina police chief on the very day he'd been discharged from the Army on February 12, 1946. While still in uniform he was brutally and viciously attacked just hours after boarding a Greyhound bus for his journey home and it would be the last time he would be able to see. His only crime, asking the bus driver to stop so that he could use the restroom,

The Boys From New York

I left Trenton when I was twenty-five and chanced to meet "The Boys From New York." These boys were men I met inside of life's transforming process and program that led us to freedom from a self induced destructive lifestyle that allowed each of us to share our God given talents with the world and especially our children. Yet this gift of life did not and could not and would not stop the dying.

I spent more than twenty years of my life with these dudes. We met at a time in our lives when we found each other in a moment of a serious dilemma for each of us. Together we watched each other rise from the ashes of our own ruin. We supported one another through a transformational process that can only be described as the miraculous process of the changing of our lives. We became "Brothers In Recovery." Like the Boys from Trenton these brothers had done all of the things that their brethren from my hometown had done and had visited many of the same kind of places and spaces who found themselves trapped inside of a funhouse that gradually transformed itself into a house of horrors; in fact a haunted house, that have devoured too many black boys and men from everywhere inside of this chronic pandemic that continues to plague us as a group throughout the width and the breadth of this nation.

The Boys from New York, unlike so many of the Boys from Trenton who never found their way out to freedom, yet nonetheless, in spite of their recovery, our recovery, the dying too early, too soon and too young syndrome has continued to prevail..

Grover, Woody, Talib. Malcolm, Malik, Tony, John "K" Key, Mike "G" Gilchrist, Michael Anderson, Garnett Wilson, Lenny B, Jamil, Bashir, Abduz Sabor, Westchester Mike, Addie "Yusef" White, Little Melvin,

Archie, Goat, Lucky, Ronnie C, Ernie, Rockman, Michael B, Mike K, Vaughn, Carl "Akil" Crawford, Tommy Washington, Lil Herman, Jihad and Jeffrey Walker. One of the culprit diseases for these deaths is HIV, ten of the men named here died of A.I.D.S and the other growing and progressive morbidity factor is liver disease caused, most likely, by untreated Hepatitis C.

Goat-"NewYawk"

Lenny B.

Abduz Sabor, Me and Grover

John K

Jamil, John K, Bashir and BIR Brothers, Mac, Rockman,

Malcolm

Yusef with Roy

Jihad, Abduz & Malik New "Yawk"

Ernie aka Kalif

Garnett "G" Wilson

Malcolm and John
Little Melvin

Michael with Sarah

Carl aka Akil

(right to left) Garnett and Lenny gone but not forgotten, me, Boone, Nat, Gerald and Roy, kneeling, 7 of the 12 "New Yawk"

IT IS IN PROFOUND SORROW
THAT WE ANNOUNCE THE PASSING OF

JEFFREY WALKER

SUNRISE NOVEMBER 16, 1957 SUNSET FEBURARY 6, 2019

VIEWING & FUNERAL
MONDAY, FEBRUARY 18TH 2019
VIEWING 2PM - 6PM | FUNERAL 6PM - 7PM
[at]
Lawrence H. Woodward Funeral Home
1 Troy Avenue
Brooklyn, NY 11213

REPASS
7pm - 10pm
29 Claver Place | Brooklyn, NY 11238

BENEDICTION & BURIAL
TUESDAY, FEBRUARY 19TH AT 9AM

FINAL RESTING PLACE
Pinelawn Memorial Park & Garden Mausoleums
Farmingdale, LI

MEMORIAL SERVICE
One year anniversary

Celebrating the Life of

Yusef Adie White

SUNRISE: June 24, 1945 **SUNSET: June 30, 2014**

Wednesday, July 22, 2015
6 PM- 8 PM

Argus Community, Inc.
760 East 160th Street, Bronx, NY 10456

Officiated by:
Imam Abukarriem Shabazz

John K. and Jamil

Tony

Robert Philly from the 'R'

Gil Redman Philly The ‘R'

Home Going Service
For
Jeffrey Aaron Seals

SUNRISE December 14, 1956 SUNSET February 23, 2

Jeffrey Seals Philly The 'R'

During the course of this life journey I was blessed to be hired as the Program Director for Ready, Willing & Able-Philadelphia aka the 'R,' a ten year rewarding experience that produced ten straight championship years of uninterrupted success. I had a God ordained opportunity to be an eyewitness to the miraculous process of the changing of the lives of hundreds of men. Men who'd been where I'd been, seen what I'd seen, did what I'd done and survived all of it yet in the aftermath too many of them would also die. It is an experience for which I am and will always be eternally grateful. Yet through this lens year after year men died; young men, of heart attacks, complications of diabetes, drug poisonings, vascular blood clots, strokes, young men in their mid to late forties an early fifties. The question is why?

Robert

Aaron Hutchins an 'R' Philly Boy

The 'Boys' from Philly present an illuminating and striking trajectory as their deaths give a view through the lens of etiology as it rest on the causes of early and premature death of African American men. The most striking commonality of the Philly 'Boys' are the ages at which they died. Nearly all of them died at midlife between the ages of 45 and less than 55 years of age. They leave a solid footprint as to the fact; like so many of the 'Boys' from Trenton, who died before they were 60 years of age. The only "Philly Boy" to live to age 60 and beyond was Al Robinson.

Al Robinson at the “R” with Big Rodney Woods and
The Philly Boys are an illuminating portrait of heart disease, cancer, stroke, drug poisoning and suicide.

54% 12:18 PM

Look at yall!! 😁😁😁 nice pic family — with **Ricky Thomas**.

Like Comment Share

Horace Clay (center) an 'R' Philly Boy

The *Philly Boys* died at ages that lend factual credence and consistency to the LCOD and the YPLL before age 65 for African American men and the the lethargic climb of our life expectancy and the fact that every other group, including African American women, live to an older age than do "black males." In fact, when African American women and men marry and do so "until death do they part," she will live; nearly, the last ten (10) years of her life without him.

We Regret To Inform You
Of The Passing Of Our Beloved:
Clyde C. Rainey, Jr.
who entered into rest on
Tuesday, February 2, 2016
Funeral Service Will Be Held:
Monday, February 8, 2016
Viewing: 9:00-11:00 A.M.
Service: 11:00 A.M.
Wayland Temple Baptist Church
2500 Cecil B. Moore Avenue
Philadelphia, PA 19121
Interment: Mt. Peace Cemetery
Sorrowfully Yours,
The Rainey Family
SERVICES ENTRUSTED TO: Marvina Hudson Bolton Memorial Chapel (267) 639-9028

Almost everything including the infant mortality rates of black baby boys as they are compared to the infant mortality survival rates of black baby girls, gives even more insight at the very beginning of our lives. Add to this the fact that historically black male babies have been born at twice the rates of black female babies yet by the time they reach age eighteen;

these numbers are reversed, black girls outnumber black boys by two to one. Why? Because the dying of black boys starts at our very beginning and along the way it; our dying, is exacerbated by an unprecedented increase in the suicide of teenage black boys between the ages of 15-19 and continues in an unprecedented fashion for those young adults 20-24 years of age. The latter stands next to homicide which is a LCOD of for the same age group, both of which have their nexus to the chronicity of trauma that pervades the lives of people in the African American community, a chronic "continuing traumatic stress disorder because there is no post!"

While I appreciate good reporting, it is disheartening; at least to this writer, that those who record the numbers of us, black men, who are missing fail miserably in accounting for the causal factors that begins at conception and continues to run along the spectrum of cradle to grave, that gives no accounting to the islands of of third world healthcare within a continent of first world affluence. The schisms of disparities at every single juncture of excess and premature death of our group, of my friends, of my and our children does not happen to us as men because all too many of us die long before we become men. These stellar reports, including the New York Times' "1.5 Black Men are Missing," give no account to the "Adverse Childhood Experiences" (ACE) over the course of the first eighteen years of life that are associated with and lead to the onset of chronic health problems including heart disease, cancers, diabetes, substance use disorders including alcohol, unintentional injuries, homicides, mental health disorders, depression, anxiety, suicide, fratricide, gendercide, genocide and the killing of ourselves for nothing! And add to this; taking Chicago into account, that there are no trauma centers available in the areas where gun violence is at its highest.

"Our generation died before we were born. Our generation died when our fathers were born!"
Quote from Aundrey Bruno
Thug Life in DC, HBO Documentary, 1998

Bobby and Marcell

Gil, Marcell and Sam
Both Gil (left) and Sam (right) died as a result of experiencing massive heart attacks.

According to the most recent Center for Disease Control and Prevention's National Vital Statistics Reports, Volume 66, Number 6, November 27, 2017, the Leading Causes of Death (LCOD) for "Black Males" in the United States, 2014 are as follows:

1. Heart Disease
2. Cancer
3. Unintentional Injuries
4. Stroke
5. Homicide
6. Diabetes
7. Chronic lower respiratory disease
8. Kidney disease
9. Septicemia

10. Influenza & pneumonia

Yet the LCOD for black boys and men across age groups is astonishing, particularly where homicide is concerned. The data demonstrates that homicide's trajectory as a LCOD is present beginning at age one (1) through age (54) fifty-four. Homicide for black boys and men is the 2nd, 4th, 2nd, 1st, 1st, 1st, 3rd and 7th LCOD for ages 1-4, 5-9, 10-14, 15-19, 20-24, 25-34, 35-44 and 45-54, respectively, Based on our collective Life Expectancy; as a group; 71.9 years, means that homicide tracks us; we are at risk of being murdered, for 75% of our lives!

"But why 'follow me?' Why not 'go before?'
Because some of my enemies are in the rear; they attack me from behind, There are foes in my yesterdays which can give me fatal wounds. They can stab me in my back! If I could only get away from my past!Its guilt dogs my steps. Its sins are forever at my heels. I have turned my face toward the Lord, but my yesterdays pursue me like a relentless hound!"
(An excerpt from the 23rd Psalms of David)

Homicide pursues us like a relentless hound chasing us for nearly all of our collective lives, catching up with us before we can barely run and when we have learned to run its bullets catches up with us shooting us in the back. It is killing us in the earliest years of our development snuffing out tens of thousands of our lives before we've had the chance to grow into men! What a sad legacy for us to leave to nobody, for there will be none of us left and it seems as if even God can't help us!

"I will die before my time, I already feel the shadows depth and have come to grips with the possibility and wipe the last tears from my eyes."

"Bury me and send me to my rest, headlines reading murdered to death!"
Tupac Shakur

Depression caused by trauma has its nexus to the never ending traumatic experiences that occur in our communities everyday. It doesn't matter whether or not you are a law abiding citizen with a legal right to carry a firearm or an undercover police officer who happens to be an African American/Black, or an unarmed teenager running away from the police, a member of a gang, living and being at home in one's own apartment or being that good guy with a gun, who just happens to be ***Black!***

Heart disease is the leading cause of death for all Americans as it is for black men in America yet what is even more astonishing is that even though we make up just under six (6%) percent of the nation's population we experience the highest rate of death due to heart disease than any other group in America. And the latter is a "drop in the bucket" when it comes to the morbidity (disease) and mortality (death) disparities associated with our dying. What do we know? We know this, Cancer is the second LCOD for all Americans yet like heart disease black men lead the nation in the rate of death as it regards the number one cancer killer, lung cancer black women; as aforementioned, die before all women in America, lead all women in the rate of death due to heart disease, breast and cervical cancers and in a more recent health disparity outcome black women are four times as likely to die giving childbirth as their white counterparts.

Black men lead the nation in the rate of death due to lung cancer caused by cigarette smoking and when it comes to Prostate Cancer black men; African Americans,living in the United States of America, have the highest rate of prostate cancer incidence and the highest rate of prostate cancer mortality (death) than any group of men on the planet earth. And when it comes to HIV, Homicide and Lung Cancer caused by cigarette smoking, respectively nobody else even comes close in any of the aforementioned categories. HIV was a prominent leading cause of death for the boys from New York and for decades had become the LCOD for those of us 25-44. As has been documented in earlier pages including the list of boys from Trenton, suicide also has its place and increasingly African American male juveniles, teenagers, adolescents and young adults are ending their lives by suicide at unprecedented rates, having

become the 3rd LCOD for Black youth (Lincoln et. al, 2012). Black youth suicide is akin to that of hypertension; the silent killer, is a quiet epidemic. I recently heard someone say, "imagine killing ourselves when living in the U.S. means dying early anyway." Imagine that the real LCOD for
Black people in America is being Black!

Unintentional injuries; accidents, including firearm deaths and their adverse effects are LCOD death starting at the very beginning of our lives. For decades we have led the nation in the rate of death due to "pedestrian mishaps," drowning, falling and casualties of fires. As it regards "pedestrian mishaps," it simply means that we are hit and killed by buses, cars, motor bikes, and trains compared to all other groups living in America.

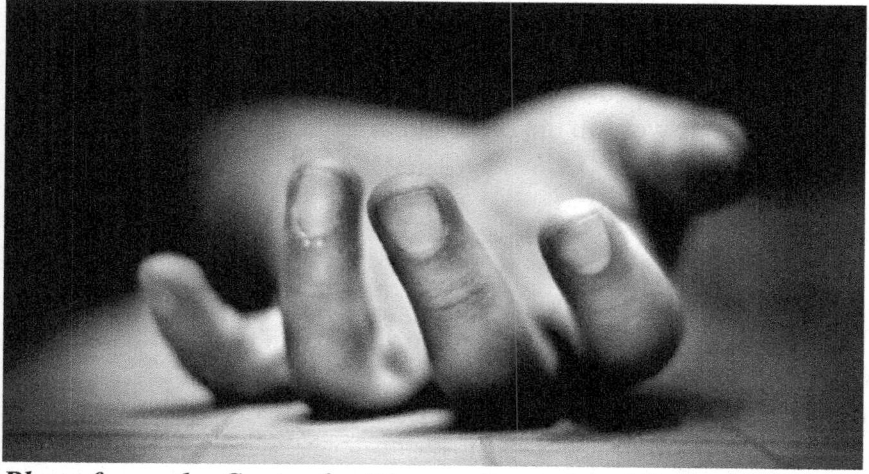

Photo from: the Center for Disease Control and Prevention.

Chapter Eight: What Can We Do?

Learn and practice the art and principles of MA'AT:

Balance,

Harmony,

Order,

Propriety,

Reciprocity and

Justice Making, blending these with the "Four Agreements:"

1. *Be Impeccable with your word*

a, speak with integrity
b. say only what you mean
c. avoid using the word to speak against yourself or to gossip about others
d. use the power of Your word in the direction of truth and love

2. ***Don't take anything personally***

a. Nothing others do is because of you
b. What others say or do is a projection of their own reality, their own dream
c. When you are immune to the opinions and actions of others you won't be the victim of needless suffering

3. ***Don't make assumptions***

a. Find the courage to ask questions and to express what you really want
b. Communicate with others as clearly as you can to avoid misunderstanding

c. With just this one agreement, you completely transform your life

4. **Al***ways do your Best*

Your best is going to change from moment to moment; it will be different when you are healthy as opposed to sick.
Under any circumstance simply do your best, and you will avoid self judgement, self abuse, and regret.

Make it to the Doctor/Regularly

Know Your Numbers (blood pressure, eye pressure, glucose-A1C, prostate PSA, weight,

Take Care of the Heart

Early Screenings for Prostate, Lung, Colon and Liver Disease/Cancers

Be in tune with your Emotional Intelligence

Avail ourselves to Trauma Informed Care and Practices: Learn the 3 R's, Realize, Recognize and Respond;

1. **Tr**auma has a widespread impact, it is real and can be both chronic and life altering yet there are pathways to recovery

2. There are signs and symptoms of trauma both physical and emotional including increased heart beat, tiredness/fatigue/lethargy, denial, anger, sadness, emotional outburst and depression

Develop and/or return to "How to Eat to Live" Practices.
SuperFoods (apples, avocado, sweet potato, spinach, tomatoes, oats, eggs, kale, wild salmon tuna, sardines, extra virgin olive oil, lean cuts of meat,

nuts, an array of green leafy vegetables), clean eating, refrain from eating processed foods, clean and superfoods are found at the outer circle of most supermarkets

Refrain from Tobacco Use

Exercise regularly: Create exercise groups

Stop the use of illicit drugs and moderate or eliminate alcohol consumption.

Ten Keys to Life: A Healthy Prostate

1. Decrease the intake of all red meats to avoid chemicals and hormones
2. Reduce fat and cholesterol in the daily diet.
3. Avoid insecticide laden fruits and vegetables.
4. Eat more organically grown vegetables and fruits
5. Eat ample amounts of nuts which supply (much needed) fatty acids.
6. Avoid beer, which is a form of alcohol that activates the hormone testosterone which stimulates the growth of the prostate
7. Take 100 mgs. of zinc daily along with B-Complex Vitamins, selenium and vitamin D3
8. Take 200 mgs. of Saw Palmetto Berry Extract twice daily. Saw Palmetto (an herb) has been found to decrease the size of the prostate.
9. One tablespoon of flaxseed oil daily will help keep the prostate healthy
10. Consult your physician before starting any diet regimen and have an adequate prostate examination inclusive of a Prostate Specific Antigen (PSA) test.
11. Cook with Extra Virgin Olive Oil

Global/Universal Harm Reduction Prevention Campaign:

- Community First Aid & Safety Instructors (CPR, Standard First Aid)
- Asthma Control Educators Instructors & Practices
- Blood Pressure Monitors Initiative
- Violence Prevention Instructors Initiative
- Prenatal Care Monitors Initiative
- Immune System Enhancement Initiative
- Mentor to Mentor Initiative (Mentors also need Mentors)
- Day Round Playground Initiative (Guardians of our Children at Promise)
- Godfather Initiative
- The Symposium Chest Initiative
- Organ Donor Initiative
- Trauma Informed Education and Practices
- Stop The Bleed

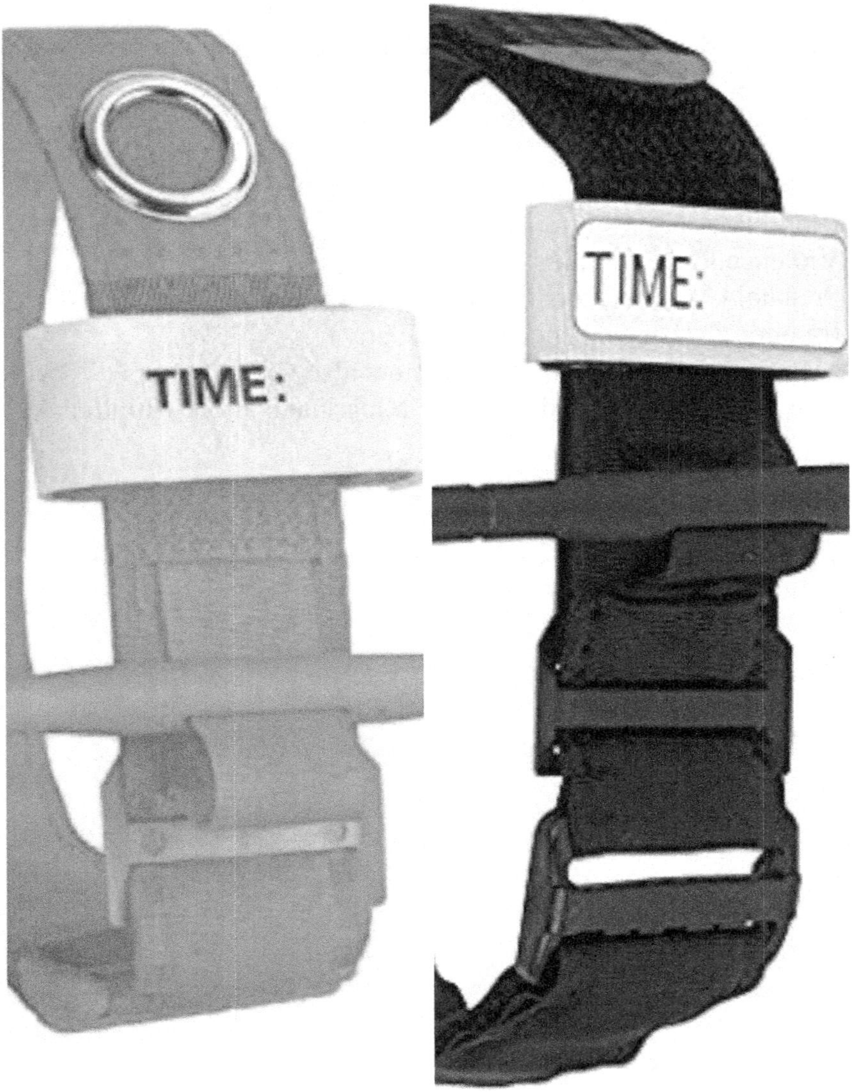

This book as it began is written to remember the memories and the joys of the "Boys…., to keep their spirits alive in the past and well into the future. Seems as I grow older the memories of the past grow closer and feel warmer and thus I write to celebrate our lives, the little boys we once were, somebody's children, children of a city, one where any of us were or could have been born. I want to encourage the rest of us, those that are left of us to revisit the richness of our past and who and what we loved and still love about it.

This book has been written from my memory and as such this treatise may not recall so much but it begs of you, the reader, to remember what I cannot and did not herein and to fill in the gaps that have been left between these pages and to share the memories and recollections of your own by writing to leave a recorded legacy and stories that have been begging to be told.

Thus, it is my hope that the readers from Trenton will fill in the gaps through social media postings and for those of you who I have met and fell in love with along the the way in New York City, the town where I lived longer than I have lived anywhere and for those of you from the "Jawn," the City of Brotherly and Sisterly Love, a place where I both lived and worked and where the bones of my father lie, I also beg of you to add your voice by placing it inside of the public square.

.... "They shall grow not old, as we that are left grow old; age shall not weary them, nor the years condemn; At the going down of the sun and in the morning, we will remember them."
For the Fallen by Laurence Binyon

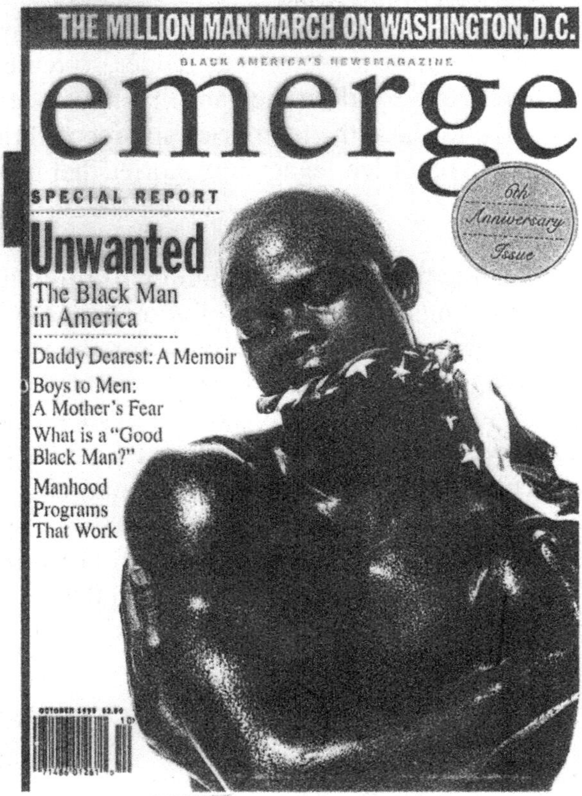

THE MILLION MAN MARCH ON WASHINGTON, D.C.
BLACK AMERICA'S NEWSMAGAZINE
emerge
6th Anniversary Issue
SPECIAL REPORT
Unwanted
The Black Man in America
Daddy Dearest: A Memoir
Boys to Men: A Mother's Fear
What is a "Good Black Man?"
Manhood Programs That Work

It is my ultimate hope and vision that we come together wherever we are to Walk. Ride and Run for Our Lives in Cities across America. That we stand up and declare that we have seen and we have had enough!

We have the ability to stem this horrible pandemic, a siege that happening to us everyday, one in which we are participants and are experiencing outcomes we never imagined, nor did we ask for. This is a national Public Health Crisis of epic and immense proportions and there is no one else to help us but us; "FUBU," (FOR US BY US)! To be locked in perpetual " Continuing Traumatic Stress Because There is No Post" ought to be intolerable and it is unconscionable and immoral.

It is imperative that we take the Gag out of our mouths and speak up. To this point, the point of our dying, we are all too often just standing around and sitting in the bleachers, watching ourselves die while being spectators in our own war.

"We must stop being spectators in our own war! To continue to be spectators is to be collaborators and conspirators in our collective demise!"

We ought rebel against living in this strange freedom freedom that we have all to often embraced and internalized and sadly, it is and always has been, killing us!

"It's a strange freedom to be adrift in the world of men, without a sense of anchor anywhere. Always there is the need for mooring, the need to have a firm grip on something that is rooted and will not give, the urge to be accountable to someone to know that beyond the individual himself there is an answer that must be given and cannot be denied. The very spirit of a person tends to panic from the desolation of going nameless up and down the streets of others minds where no salutation greets and no friendly recognition makes secure. being passed over as if of no account and of no meaning is to be made into a faceless thing and not a person, it is better to be the complete victim of an anger unrestrained and a rath which knows no bounds. to be torn asunder without mercy encountered, or to be battered to a pulp by an angry violence than to be passed over as if one were not here. Here at least one is dealt with, encountered, vanquished, or overwhelmed but not ignored It's a strange freedom to be adrift in the world of men, going up and down the streets of other's minds where no sign is given to mark the place that one calls one's own, it's a strange freedom and for such of us from the acquiescence of the heart, even death is not dying." *By Howard Thurman*

gofundme
Eradicating Premature Death AAMUSOL

"WE ARE WHAT WE THINK, HAVING BECOME WHAT WE THOUGHT"

You were a light in my life, a warrior boy with who I fought both with and against. You were like me, a lets get it done kind of boy and man, go hard or go home! We dabbled in street entrepreneurship together, drank gallons of Hennessy at the.V Bar, Charlie Harpers, The Monument Lounge and Paulie's Corner. You were from every part of our town; Trenton, you were from North Trenton, Wayne Avenue, where we first fought as 12 year olds, you were from South Trenton and Wilbur Section, you came back to North Trenton and spent some time living in West Trenton. We rocked the rock at Kingsbury and did the same thing at 730 Pennington Avenue at Donald's crib. We put our lives on the line together and when I was injured badly you didn't leave me even at the risk of your own peril. You always showed up, we always knew when you were in the room, you were always colorful, always loud, always bodacious, always alive with spirit and you always told me the truth. The most remarkable thing about you is that you never let your setbacks kill your spirit. You were only one of few people who could cuss me out and it be received by me with love. You were always loyal and you were always my friend. It seemed like all of this happened over a long period of time yet when I think about it, actually it was a very short period. I am enough of a believer to believe that you; Tyrone, may have been an Angel!

Tyrone George

"The days of our years are threescore years and ten and if by reason of strength they be fourscore, yet their strength is labor and sorrow, and is soon cut off, and we fly away"

In MEMORIAM and SALUTATIONS

THE END?

LeeRoy Jordan

aamusol2306@gmail.com

704-835-6301

LeeRoy Jordan, Jr. is the Founder, President and CEO of Afrikan American Men United to Save Our Lives, Inc, (AAMUSOL), a grassroots movement and organization
dedicated to the uplifting of the entire black diaspora through the eradication of Excess and Premature death of Afrikan American boys 2 men. He is a Qualified Health Professional (QHP), .who for the past three decades has assisted hundreds of people in redirecting their lives. As a QHP, Mr. Jordan has an extensive background, acquired through education, training and work experience as a human services technician and program manager, chemical dependency and criminal justice practitioner, independent consultant, motivational coach/ trainer and workforce development practitioner.

Over the past 30 years Mr. Jordan has been employed as a counselor, court liaison, case manager, criminal justice advocate, supervising criminal justice advocate, assistant director of court programs, youth services director, assistant director of addiction services and director of non-profit community based organizations (CBO) in the cities of Philadelphia, Pennsylvania and New York, New York. For nearly a decade he served as an award winning Director of Ready, Willing & Able-Philadelphia, in the “City of Brotherly Love and Sisterly Affection,” in Philadelphia, serving homeless, formerly incarcerated single men, many of who present with significant histories of chemical dependency.

Mr. Jordan has worked extensively with criminal/juvenile justice populations; Persons/Children In Need of Supervision (PCINS); Pre-Trial Felony Defendants; Probationers; Parolees; Parole/Probation Violators; juvenile offenders; juvenile delinquents; jail and prisons inmates. He has advocated for alternatives to incarceration and diversions to "placement" for hundreds of individuals in criminal proceedings, parole hearings and family court hearings involving juvenile delinquents. He is recognized as a founder of El Rio, a chemical dependency treatment program; exclusively designed to provide treatment services to persons involved in the criminal justice system, operated by Osborne Treatment Services, Inc., a subsidiary of the Osborne Association, Inc., in the South Bronx, New York.

Mr. Jordan has been a sought after speaker, trainer, workshop leader and instructor. He has delivered trainings for more than one hundred organizations around the nation from New York City to New Orleans, La., from Atlanta, Georgia to Cincinnati, Columbus, Cleveland, Dayton, Elyria, Lorain, Oberlin and Toledo, Ohio, to Salem and Springfield, Mass., to Woonsocket, Rhode Island and from Washington, D.C. to San Juan, Puerto to Philadelphia, Pa. He has presented in the halls of The University of the District of Columbia in Washington, D.C., Columbia, University in New York City to Temple University in Philadelphia at such esteemed conferences as the National Conference on Women in Prison hosted at Columbia University in New York City and the annual ***Beyond the Walls: Prison Health Care and Reentry Summits*** presented by Philadelphia FIGHT hosted at Temple University and the

Pennsylvania Convention Center in Philadelphia, Pennsylvania, respectively, 2007-2013.

Mr. Jordan has taught at the Summer Institute for Advanced Social Work Practices & Addiction Studies at the University at Buffalo, State University of New York. He has also taught as an Adjunct Instructor at Hostos Community College, a school of City College of New York, located in the Bronx, New York.

Some of the highlights of his career as a presenter include pre-conference and keynote presentations at national and international conferences including the national ***Sanctuary Network Conference in White Plains, NY, in 2013; Delaware Devoted Dads Conference at the Dover Downs Casino Hotel, Dover, Delaware, 2010; Counseling and Treating People of Color Conference: An International Perspective, San Juan, Puerto Rico, 1999 and The Black Alcoholism and Addiction Institute in Atlanta, Georgia in 1998-2000,*** respectively.

Mr. Jordan has also presented before the New Jersey Judiciary Drug Court Training Conference under the auspices of the Administration of the Courts Criminal Practice Division held at the Law Center, New Brunswick, New Jersey.

He has written articles and has been written about or quoted in the New York Times, The World Tribune, Harlem Overheard Youth News and Channel 6 ABC News Affiliate; CBS 3 KYW News Radio 1060 and WURD Radio 900 AM. He wrote the first editorial article in the column ***"Message from the Elders,"*** for ***Harlem Overheard Youth*** News, the largest youth circulated youth news paper of its kind in the nation, during the 1990's. During his tenure as Director of Ready, Willing & Able-Philadelphia, he was featured in the Public Television, WHYY Philadelphia "Coming of Age" Series and he was also featured in MIND TV's (Philadelphia) short film documentary about Ready, Willing & Able.

Mr. Jordan is a health care advocate and a Chemical Dependency Professional trained and certified in the addictions. He is a Certified Addiction Counselor (CAC), Certified Addiction Specialist, Credentialed Alcoholism and Substance Abuse Counselor (CASAC), National Certified Addiction Counselor II (NCAC II), Certified Gang Specialist, Certified Violence Prevention Specialist and a Certified Violence Prevention Educator.

He is the architect of ***"The African American Male Health Care Horo-Caust: Dying Not For A Cause But Because,"*** an in-depth, informative and thought provoking "Lifeshop" that was presented in its entirety for the first time on the campus of Oberlin College; the first college in the United States to admit African Americans, in Oberlin, Ohio in 1995. Other workshops include ***"What Killed Tupac Shakur? Utilizing the Power of Gangsta Rap Toward Violence Prevention; Fatherhood Then and Now; Substance Abuse Treatment in A Criminal Justice Context;The Gang-Thang and others.*** He also authored the forward; ***"The Malt Liquor Marketing Madness-New York City Style," for "Message NA Bottle-The 40oz. SCANDAL: The SCANDAL CONTINUES, VOLUME 2, written by Alfred "Coach" Powell.***

Three of the most riveting and thought provoking and moving "Lifeshops"d presentations; ***"Both Ends of the Spectrum: Standing Your Ground, The Law, Mass Murder and The Gun Lobby In Black and White: The Application of S.E.L.F (Safety, Emotions, Loss & Future) Framework of The Sanctuary Model," "Dismantling Teaching Our Children to Kill: Understanding the Connection Between Adverse Childhood Experiences (ACE) and the Pathology of Homicide Affecting and Effecting Children and Young people in Philadelphia and the Nation; "Murder in Philadelphia: Understanding The Murder of African American Boys 2 Men And The Pathology of "Continuing Traumatic Stress Because There is No Post!"*** at the Philadelphia Fight Beyond The Prison Walls: Health Care and Reentry Summits, 2014, '13 and '12, respectively, and Dismantling Teaching Our Children to Kill, presented at the National Sanctuary Network Conference in 2013.

Mr. Jordan has also provided services to organizations in other cities including the New York Theological Seminary; Urban Minority Alcohol and Drug Outreach Programs of Ohio; Institute For The Prevention and Eradication of Violence of Washington, D.C.; Lorraine County Alcohol and Drug Abuse Program of Elyria, Ohio; National Black Alcoholism and Addictions Council and Morehouse College School of Medicine, Atlanta, Georgia; the NAACP of Woonsocket, Rhode Island; ADAHMS Board of Montgomery County of Dayton, Ohio; Salem College, Salem, Massachusettes; Drug Policy Foundation; The Harm Reduction Institute, and the Economic Opportunities Commission of Nassau County. While living and working in New York City he provided consultant services and training to the Harlem Children's Zone (formerly the Rheedlen Centers for Children and Families); Big Brother and Big Sisters; The Women's Prison Association; The American Red Cross, The Administration for Children's Services, The Northern Manhattan Perinatal Partnership; Palladia, Inc., The Federation of Protestant Welfare Agencies, Inc.; The College of New Rochelle,; Hostos Community College (as an Adjunct Instructor); Erasmus High School of Brooklyn, New York; Roosevelt High School of the Bronx, New York; New York Council on Adoptable Children; Grandparents Advocacy Project, Inc.; Jackie Robinson, Center for Physical Culture of Brooklyn, New York; Brookwood Child Care of Brooklyn, New York; The New York Theological Seminary and a host of others including the DeLasalle School in Philadelphia, PA.

Mr. Jordan has been awarded citations from the Rhode Island House of Representatives by the State of Rhode Island and Providence Plantations; The Department of Services for Children, Youth and Families and the Delaware's Devoted Dad's Summit by the State of Delaware; The Town of Hempstead, New York; The Economic Opportunity Commission of Nassau County, Inc., New York; Waters Memorial African Methodist Episcopal Church, The Oasis of African Methodism of Philadelphia, Pennsylvania and a the City Council of Philadelphia, Proclamation for the award winning work as the Director of Ready, Willing & Able-Philadelphia.

Mr. Jordan, for nearly his entire career, has been an advocate for pretrial felony defendants including juvenile offenders, the formerly incarcerated and returning citizens in two of the nation's major metropolis', New York City and Philadelphia, PA, Over the course of a period of seventeen years he worked for two of the nation's largest Criminal Justice Agencies, The Court Employment Project, a program of The Center for Alternative Sentencing and Employment Services and The Osborne Association, Inc, of New York City, respectively. He has served as an advocate for Alternatives to Re-Incarceration, advocating for the restoration of parole supervision for technical parole violators, writing extensive revocation memorandums and participating in parole violation hearing proceedings. During his tenure at the Osborne Association, he held multiple position including the Assistant Director of Youth Court Services and the Assistant Director of Youth Services. He spent hundreds of hours inside of the Family Court of New York City advocating for Diversions for youth having been arrested for drug sale and/or possession and adjudged to be "Juvenile Delinquent."

Mr. Jordan has been inside of the prison walls around the nation. He has accompanied the former Executive Director, Mr. Robert Gangi, of the Correctional Association of New York on a fact finding mission at the Green Correctional located in upstate New York. He has also assisted in conducting a four day "Quality Improvement Review" for the Phoenix House Foundation at the Yorktown Program in Yorktown Hieghts, New York. He has also visited and been a guest speaker at the Orient Correctional Facility in Ohio, the House of Detention for Men and the Adolescent Detention and Reception Center at the New York City Department of Corrections on Rikers Island, New York. He has also been invited as a group facilitator to conduct a exploratory group session about violence with women inmates at the maximum security prison at Bedford Hills, New York and for nearly a decade he work in the Children's Center run by the Osborne Association, Inc., at one of America's oldest maximum security prisons; Sing-Sing Correctional Institution in Ossining, New York. While at Sing-Sing, Mr. Jordan conducted workshops and group think tanks with inmates in the "Family Works" program in an effort to provide assistance and support to fathers who were incarcerated, some who were serving life sentences.

One of the highlights of his esteem career, of which his most proud, is his work on behalf, of and in the "deportation" case of Angela. In 2003, while working for the Educational Alliance, Inc., in New York City, where he served as the Assistant Site Director of Pride Site II, a coed addiction treatment program located on the Lower East Side of Manhattan. It was there he met Angela, a client in the program. Angela was an immigrant from the Caribbean/Trinidad, who sometime in 1991 was convicted of a drug offense for which she served time.

While attempting to renew her Green Card at 26 Federal Plaza in lower Manhattan she was arrested and detained for deportation and immediately transferred to a deportation detention center in York, Pennsylvania. Having consulted with immigration attorneys in past cases he immediately contacted them and over the next few weeks he would also consult with immigration authorities in York, Pennsylvania and relying on his wealth of experience having written pre-sentence memorandums, pre-revocation memorandums, bail applications and hundreds of progress reports to the courts, he wrote what he called ***"A Waiver of Deportation"*** on Angela's behalf to the Office of Homeland Security, that was presented to the Immigration Judge on the morning of Angela's first deportation hearing since being held in detention. That afternoon, Angela was released. She said that the Judge literally told her that "nobody leaves here," which was what she had also been told by her fellow detainees. Over the next several months, Mr. Jordan would accompany Angela to Immigration Court hearings until he left the organization. In 2008 he was contacted by Angela who informed him that after years of litigation and court proceedings, she had finally been granted permission by the United States Government and its Office of Homeland Security to continue to remain in the United States as a "Naturalized Citizen."

In 2010 Mr. Jordan was summoned by the Mayor of Philadelphia; Michael A. Nutter, as one of Philadelphia's leaders and stakeholders, commissioned to be a member of the Mayor's 2020 Re-Entry Summit, a three day think tank of some of the best minds in the City of Philadelphia including law enforcement, city government, corrections, probation, business leaders and non-profits to craft a visionary paradigm that would be serve the city's citizens returning to the City of Philadelphia, after having served periods of incarceration in the Commonwealth's prison system. He served on a panel that included Charles Ramsey, Commissioner of the Philadelphia Police Department, Louis Giorla, Commissioner of the Philadelphia Prison System, Everett Gillison, the former Deputy Mayor of Public Safety and the Mayor's Chief of Staff. Before relocating to Charolette, North Carolina, he was named to the city of Philadelphia's Mayoral Opioid Task Force under the auspices of the office of the Honrorable Mayor Jim Kenny and under the leadership of Pamela McClenton.

Made in the USA
Columbia, SC
19 February 2020

88151132R00207